"I DON'T WANT TO TALK ABOUT THAT PLACE NOW."

"Talk about what place, Bill?"

"Grandville."

"Grandville? Isn't that the State Mental Institution?"

"Yes, but I'm out now. Ole Bill's out now and I'm doin' fine. And I got me some real hair, like a real good man. I got me a job and I do all the clean-up, and I'm not gonna get in trouble no more."

The door swung open and Bev came in. "Barry? You ready?" She moved to the sink and took Barry's arm. "Hi, Bill."

"Hi," he answered matter-of-factly.

"Well, nice to talk to you, Bill," Barry said.

Bill frowned and pointed his scouring pad at Bev. "Is that sweetie your wife?"

Barry smiled. "Yeah, this sweetie is my wife."

Bill gazed solemnly at the two of them. "You're a lucky guy," he said. Then he turned back to his pots and pans and resumed scrubbing, rocking gently back and forth....

THE STORY OF BILL
Nothing could stop his joy for life...
or his need to be loved.

THE
STORY
OF
BILL

Robert Weverka

A novelization based on the teleplays of *Bill*
and *Bill On His Own*

by

Barry Morrow and
Corey Blechman

BANTAM BOOKS
TORONTO · NEW YORK · LONDON · SYDNEY

An Alan Landsburg Production
A Reeves Communications Company
THE STORY OF BILL
A Bantam Book / December 1983

ISBN 0-553-24094-3

Published simultaneously in the United States and Canada

Bantam Books are published by Bantam Books, Inc. Its trade-
mark, consisting of the words "Bantam Books" and the por-
trayal of a rooster, is Registered in U.S. Patent and Trademark
Office and in other countries. Marca Registrada. Bantam
Books, Inc., 666 Fifth Avenue, New York, New York 10103.

PRINTED IN THE UNITED STATES OF AMERICA

O   0 9 8 7 6 5 4 3 2 1

BILL

I

The man playing Santa Claus was huge; a great balloon-sized man whose red velvet-covered belly bulged out so far he had no lap at all. As he hoisted the children to his knees he threw his head back, eyes twinkling, and laughed with a deep booming voice that was as jolly as all the Christmases in the world. He promised dolls and video games and wagons and bicycles and train sets, and with a sly smile he extracted promises of good behavior from all his squirming, wide-eyed supplicants.

The line of anxious children and reassuring parents extended along the low picket fence and out beyond the central fountain of the shopping mall. The happy sound of Christmas carols drifted over the splash of the fountain, and the air was filled with the smells of popcorn and candy and leather and perfume and cheese and spices.

Bill Sackter was enjoying every minute of it. He had wandered into the mall in the late afternoon, and moved unhurriedly along from shop to shop, his hands deep in his pockets, smiling happily, being jostled by the crowds as he paused to look in the display windows. He had wandered into toy shops and delicatessens and video arcades, and made his way through all the aisles of the two department stores.

Now he stood outside the picket fence surrounding Santa Claus and the four styrofoam reindeer, grinning broadly, clasping his stubby hands together and rising on his toes each time Santa hoisted another child to his knee. His eyes grew as large as those of the children, and with every "Ho, ho, ho," from Santa Claus, he echoed the sounds under his breath and grinned at the spectators around him. It was a wonderful show, and his eyes twinkled with delight as each child stepped forward.

He was a short, stocky man with a crooked smile under a thatched hairpiece that looked like a dark haystack sprouting over his fringes of gray hair. And like the smaller children he was watching, there was an innocence and wonderment in his eyes that could quickly change from fear and anxiety to delight and joy.

"Ho, ho, ho," Santa Claus boomed as he lowered a three-year-old girl to the floor and watched her run to her mother.

Bill grinned and tilted his head back. "Ho, ho, ho," he said almost as loud as Santa Claus. He turned his grin to the crowd, and then to the tiny blonde-haired girl staring up from beside him. "Ho, ho, ho," he boomed out again.

The girl hunched her shoulders and smiled shyly. She was a pretty little girl wearing a green jumpsuit and a red ribbon in her blonde curls.

"Merry Christmas," Bill said to her. The words had a slurred sound, as if Bill's mouth were half full of water.

The little girl started to giggle, and her mother glared at Bill. Then the woman grabbed her daughter's hand and strode away.

Bill gazed curiously after them. "Merry Christmas," he called out again. "Merry Christmas!" But neither the girl nor her mother looked back.

The other parents were all looking at him now; some smiling hesitantly, the others frowning.

Bill sensed the doubts and tensions that suddenly charged the air, an awkwardness he had felt many times before when people stared at him. It always confused and frightened him a little. He nodded and smiled sheepishly back at them, well aware of what they were thinking. He was just a crack-minded old man. He didn't have any real hair on his head, and he couldn't read or write, or tell time, or do a lot of the things other people could do.

He slid his hands deep into his overcoat pockets and moved on.

It was growing dark when he walked out of the department store and shuffled his way across the crowded parking lots. An icy wind was blowing at his back and he tightened the collar of his overcoat. But the warm memories of the Christmas carols and Santa Claus's laughter still washed over him. He grinned and tossed his head back. "Ho, ho, ho," he laughed.

He walked for two hours. But he had no sense of time. He looked at all the colorful lights, and the Christmas decorations hanging from the telephone poles, and he was careful crossing the streets. Miss Keating, the county welfare lady had taught him about that. People in Minneapolis drove fast, and he should always wait at the corners until the cars were stopped. He crossed the streets carefully and smiled at the shoppers and pedestrians and policemen and newsboys, and he looked in store windows, and watched people file in and out of tall buildings. Everybody seemed to be having a good time; smiling, hurrying along with their packages, all bundled up against the cold weather.

Several blocks past the bus station the streets were dirtier than before. The people were not dressed as nicely as in other parts of the city, and most of them were men. None of them were smiling, and they stood on the sidewalks talking to each other in low voices. There weren't any Christmas decorations in this part of the city, and the bars all had loud music that blared out into the street. It was strange, and Bill felt uncomfortable.

"Hey buddy—"

The man grabbed Bill's arm. It was not a tight

grip, but it was firm enough to turn Bill around. He was a tall, gaunt-looking man wearing a tattered old jacket over a dirty sweat shirt. He hadn't shaved for several days and his eyes were all bloodshot.

"Can you spare a quarter, buddy? I need something to eat."

Bill stared at him, remembering that he hadn't eaten for a long time himself—not since he'd left the kitchen at the country club where he worked.

"How much do you need?" he asked.

The man smiled, showing a mouthful of brown teeth. "How much you got, pal?"

Bill shrugged. Fred had given him some money, but he didn't know how much it was. It was paper money. "I don't know how much I got."

The man laughed. "Well, dig in your pocket and take a look, pal."

Bill nodded. He remembered that the money was in the righthand pocket of his pants, and he dug it out and held it up for the man to see. "That's all."

Apparently it was enough. The man grinned at him and put his arm around his shoulder, squeezing it hard as he pushed Bill through a door. Loud music was coming from the darkness inside. "That's fine, pal. We'll get something to eat, huh? A little beer, or something?"

Bill nodded, trying to see in the darkness. "All right."

"Yeah, I been lookin' for a friend like you for a long time, pal."

Bill suddenly felt warm again. It was good to have a friend, somebody to talk to.

"Is your name Marjorie Keating?" a rough male voice asked on the telephone.

"Yes, I am Miss Keating."

"This is the Minneapolis Police Department, Miss Keating. Do you know an old guy named William Sackter?"

"Bill Sackter? Yes, I know him. I'm his case worker."

"Well, we've got him down here at the police station, Miss Keating. You'd better come and get him."

Marge Keating sat patiently in the Police Department waiting room wondering how many phone calls like that she had received in the last fifteen years. A thousand? Maybe two thousand? And how many for Bill Sackter in the past two years? Twenty? Thirty? She was beginning to wonder if he might not be better off back in the home for the retarded.

The phone call had come at nine P.M., just after she had washed her hair and was looking forward to a quiet evening of watching television. So she had wrapped her head in a scarf and driven downtown, wondering why county welfare workers were not paid as well as doctors. And now, along with a dozen anxious mothers and brothers and sisters and assorted attorneys, she sat in another smelly police station waiting for good or bad news from the dungeons inside.

In theory it was a good idea to find jobs for retarded adults and send them out into the community. It certainly eased the financial burdens of taking care of them in state institutions. And it was probably good for people like Bill to have contacts with normal people. But when they ended up in jail, or were beaten up, or were taken advantage of by all kinds of deviates, you had to wonder if the benefits outweighed the complications.

"Miss Keating?"

He was a young cop with a crew cut and a freshly scrubbed face. Marge Keating stood up. "Yes."

"My name is Cunningham. You want to come with me?"

She followed him through the door into a room full of desks—manned by a skeleton crew of bored policemen. "Is Bill all right?"

"Yeah, he's okay. I guess he didn't hurt anybody but himself. You wanna have a seat? You'll have to sign these papers."

Marge sat down and signed the release forms. "Are there any charges?"

"Naw, we didn't book him. He got picked up in an alley with some other winos."

"Bill is not a wino," she said flatly.

"Yeah, well, whatever. They'll be bringin' him out in a minute."

"Bill's just slow. He can't read or write, and he can't handle money."

The young officer nodded, not really interested. There were enough murders and rapes and bank robberies every day in Minneapolis. Why should anybody care about an old man who didn't know the time of day?

Bill finally came through the door, his head down, shuffling across the room. He looked like a six-year-old boy who'd just come out of the principal's office. His dark wig, which looked silly enough under normal circumstances, was now resting on the side of his head, half covering his ear.

"I'm sorry, Miss Keating," he whimpered when he reached the desk. There was a cut on his cheekbone, and the whole right side of his face was puffed and swollen. He kept his head down as if hoping nobody would notice.

Marge took his arm and guided him through the door and across the waiting room. Once they were outside she kept him moving toward the car. "Well, Bill, what am I going to do with you?"

The question didn't seem to register. Bill was concentrating on something else. "I went with this guy in the bar," he said. "He wanted something to eat." He told the story as if it was all very puzzling, one of the world's great mysteries. "He was a nice man, and we drank some beer and ate pretzels. I like pretzels."

Marge said nothing until she got the car moving. Then she spoke very clearly and deliberately. "Bill, you've been out of Grandville long enough to know that you have to stay out of trouble. You've had a dozen different jobs...you've been arrested...you've been beaten up. And now you've done it again."

Bill nodded agreement and gave her a shy glance. "I'll try harder next time."

"Stop it, Bill."

"I'll do better next time," he said with more determination.

"If you don't stop it, Bill, there may not be a next time."

Bill frowned and pursed his lips and glanced out at the traffic. Her warning was probably too abstract for him to understand.

"Bill," she said, "I got you this job at the country club to keep you out of trouble. Remember?"

"I remember, Miss Keating. I won't be in any trouble anymore. Everything's all right now. He shook his head, then smiled as if everything were suddenly fine again. "Won't get pinched by a cop no more. Everything is hunky-dory."

"And the television," she reminded him. "I bought the television so you'd have something to do in your spare time. Why—?"

The word television brought a happy smile to his face. "Television! Oh, boy. *I Dream of Jeanie!* That's a real cutie!"

Marge sighed. She wasn't getting through to him. Maybe it was impossible. "Bill, I'm beginning to run out of patience. Any more trouble and it's back to—"

"Don't say it, don't say it!" he pleaded. He clenched his fists and closed his eyes.

"—Grandville," she said deliberately. "Do you hear me? I mean it, Bill. It's getting to the point where there'll be no other choice if you don't behave yourself."

She had pulled into the driveway of the country club, and he said nothing until she drove around the building and stopped at the back door. By then his optimism had returned. Or maybe it was determination. He smiled at her and opened the car door, his black wig still resting on his ear. "I'll be all right, Miss Keating," he said with an emphatic nod. "We're all

7

gonna be fine. You can count on it. Merry Christmas."
He shut the door and ambled toward the kitchen,
laughing merrily. "Ho, ho, ho," he said. "Merry
Christmas."

She knew the determination would not last. Very
little of what she told him ever penetrated very deeply
into his memory. Two minutes from now he would
forget their entire conversation. And tomorrow he would
wander away from the country club again and end up
God only knew where. And on her case load there
were seven other men and four women exactly like
him.

She swung the car around and headed home,
hoping none of the others were out having a night on
the town.

II

It looked like a good party. At least the music was
upbeat, and people were talking and laughing and
dancing. Barry Morrow slipped through the door and
stood at the side for a minute, scanning the crowd. The
guests were all staff members of the Minikahda Country Club, along with their husbands and wives and
friends. Four or five days before Christmas every year,
the club directors turned the facilities over to the help,
and all the maids and waitresses and groundskeepers
let their hair down and had a good time.

The logs crackling in the fireplace gave the big
room a cozy atmosphere, and the giant Christmas tree
in the corner was loaded with decorations and twinkling lights.

Bev—his wife—was nowhere in sight, and he rec-
ognized only a handful of people. Among them was the
tennis pro, a forty-year-old tanned god sitting at the bar

with a cluster of teenaged worshippers. Barry smiled and edged around the crowd.

"Hey, Barry! Merry Christmas."

The voice belonged to Fred Keller, who was moving a little unsteadily across the room, a fresh drink in his hand.

"Hi. Merry Christmas, Fred. Have you seen Bev?"

Fred gestured vaguely toward the far corner and put an arm around Barry's shoulders. "How's your old career coming along, buddy?"

It was a question Barry didn't much enjoy answering lately. Euphemistically he called himself a filmmaker. Which meant he scraped up a few dollars now and then to buy a few hundred feet of film, and then shot and edited it into great documentaries that he sent to various people around the country hoping one of them would say it wasn't too bad. Then he hoped that some kind person with good taste and judgment would send him a check to buy more film which he could use to produce an epic that would make them both a million dollars.

The "career," as Fred called it, was much like trying to become a novelist or a songwriter. No matter how good you were, you were still nothing until somebody handed you a check and made you a bona fide professional. The trick was to pretend you were confident, and that you had a hundred irons in the fire, and it was just a question of days before the postman delivered the magic envelope.

"Not too bad, Fred," he said. "I'm kind of in between at the moment."

Fred grinned at him, knowing exactly what "in between" meant. "You know what I'd do if I was you?"

"What?" Barry asked. Fred Keller was a successful stockbroker in town and his wife managed the coffee shop at the country club. If Barry ever came up with a hot idea for a film, Fred claimed to know lots of people who would be very interested in investing a good chunk

9

of cash. What Fred meant was that his friends would be interested in buying all the rights to "E.T." for a couple hundred thousand dollars.

"If I was you, old buddy, I'd go out to Hollywood. If you're gonna spend all that time making movies, why freeze your butt doin' it in Minneapolis?"

Barry nodded and slipped out of his grasp. "Yeah, sounds like a good idea. Thanks, Fred."

He skirted around the dance floor and finally spotted Bev re-stocking a cooler with soft drinks. She looked as fresh and pretty as ever.

"Hi."

She turned quickly, gave him a bright smile and wiped her hands on a towel. "Hi. How are you?"

"Incredibly ordinary. How are you? Wanna dance?"

"Sure. Who with?"

"Ha, ha," Barry said. "I'm supposed to tell the jokes in the family. Remember?"

"Sorry," she said and took his hand.

They squeezed their way onto the floor and danced at half the pace of the disco music. The six-piece band had more enthusiasm than talent, and Barry wished they would outlaw disco music—at least during the Christmas holidays. "Good party," he said.

"So far," she laughed. "The next hour will separate the drunks from the human beings. Where've you been?"

"Watching a *National Geographic* documentary about gorillas."

"Was it good?"

"It was sensational. I hated every minute of it. It made me feel like a gross amateur—like a three-year-old watching Michelangelo at work."

"Hmph. Don't put yourself down. You're at least a five-year-old."

"Ha, ha. You're really full of beans tonight, aren't you."

10

She looked up at him and smiled. "I have reason to be. I got some news today."

"What?"

"I talked to the doctor. The tests were back, and I am definitely pregnant."

Barry gave her a brief smile, then held her tighter as the wild dancers came dangerously close. "They have any idea who the father is?"

She laughed. "That's not a good joke. I think I'll have to take over the joke department."

He kissed her on top of the head. "You're gonna be too busy for that. Listen, I think it's great."

"Oh, Barry, I'm so happy." She put her head on his chest and hugged him.

"It's sensational. Listen, you worked all day, honey. Let's get out of here. Come on. Let's go somewhere and celebrate by ourselves."

She bit her lip and glanced around. "Well . . . I'm one of the hostesses. I'd better stick around awhile."

"Isn't there some place we can go where it's quiet?"

She led him off the dance floor and back to the soft drink bar. "There's a patio back there, through the kitchen. Give me about ten minutes. Okay?"

"Okay."

Barry edged around the dance floor and made his way toward the kitchen, smiling faintly to himself. It was no big surprise that he was going to be a father. Bev had been having the symptoms for two weeks now. But he was still finding it hard to grapple with all the implications. It was what almost all couples planned for. But the plans were generally focused on some vague date in the future. Aside from those who planned very carefully, he supposed it was like that for every father. But it would have been nice if his so-called "career" was a little farther along the way.

The kitchen was a jungle of stainless-steel racks and trays and ovens and serving carts. Off to the right, two men were standing by a sink that was piled high with dirty pots and pans. One of them was a tall, wiry man about forty, with stooped shoulders and tattooed arms. He was waving his hands, apparently berating the shorter man for something. Barry felt embarrassed momentarily. He glanced around searching for the back door to the patio.

"Where you been, for cryin' out loud?" the taller man said. "You're an hour late!" He pointed at the wall. "Look at that clock. What does it say?"

The short man had tied an apron around his waist. He turned on a faucet and looked at the dirty pots. "I don't like to look at clocks," he said indifferently. "Thank you very much."

His voice was strange, as if he didn't quite close his mouth when he spoke. On top of his head he was wearing a black wig that spread out in all directions like an old dust mop.

"Thank you very much," the tall man said, mimicking the other man's words. "Dimwit."

The short man winced, as if the insult had been a blow to his head. "I'll clean up real good," he said. "Clean as a whistle. I'll clean good." His voice sounded tight now, as if he were on the verge of tears.

"Yeah, you'll clean real good," the tall man sneered. "If you weren't so stupid I'd believe you. You got the brains of a half-witted two-year-old. An' I'm gonna come back and check on you every half hour, so don't go wanderin' off again. You understand?"

The short man nodded. "I unnerstan'. I won't forget."

The other man stared at him for a minute, then walked toward Barry. He smiled and shook his head, as if to tell Barry how hopeless the situation was, then continued out the door.

Barry had never heard a man speak to another one in such a degrading manner. It had sounded like something out of the Dark Ages. He watched the short man scour a pan for a minute, then he moved over to the sink. "What are you doing washing pans? There's a Christmas party going on out there."

The man frowned at him and continued scrubbing. "I'm cleaning up because..." He hesitated, as if trying to remember what he was going to say. "I'm cleaning up because Harry said to clean up. Make everything clean as a whistle."

There was a deep cut on his face, and his cheek was all swollen. Barry wondered if the tall man had beaten him up. "Why don't you clean the pans later, and join the party?"

The man solemnly shook his head. "Harry said for me to do it now. So I'm doing my cleaning now."

"Well, why don't you just tell Harry to shove it where the sun don't shine?"

The man gave him a shy glance and shook his head. "I can't do that." He scrubbed some more, then turned abruptly and thrust out a wet hand. "Bill," he said. "My name is William. Bill for short."

Barry shook the wet hand and smiled. "Well, hi, Bill. I'm Barry."

Bill nodded. "Hi, Perry."

"No, Barry."

Bill nodded again. "Perry for short."

Barry couldn't help laughing. The man seemed so childish, as if he had the mentality of a five- or six-year-old. But there was a streak of independence in him, as if he didn't want people to treat him like a five-year-old. "Yeah," Barry said. "Perry for short."

Bill seemed pleased. "Perry for short," he repeated.

"Are you the clean-up man around here?"

Bill nodded. "I'm the clean-up man. I do the clean-up work. Bill does all the clean-up. Yep."

"What happened to your face?"

The old man seemed happy to talk about his troubles, as if he'd had an adventure he was eager to tell somebody about. He rocked his head back and forth and almost sang the story. "I was downtown...and this guy come up to me and says, 'Buddy?' He didn't know my name, and I said, 'Yes.' He says, 'You wanna have a beer with me?' and I said, 'Sure, buddy, I'll have a beer with you.' And then he said, 'How would you like for me to knock your teeth out?' And I said my teeth aren't very good anyhow."

Barry waited, but apparently the story was over. Bill seemed to smile to himself, pleased with the way he'd explained things. He rinsed off the pan, set it aside, and started on another. "You gotta be careful 'bout goin' downtown," he said. "Lotta fights. Gotta be careful. Cops'll pinch you."

"Pinch you?" Barry wasn't sure if he meant "arrest you," or if somebody had really pinched him.

Bill nodded. "Then they put it on your record— that you're a low grade man." He said it as if being a "low grade man" was the worst fate anybody could imagine. "Then they might put you back in that place."

There was something fascinating about the man. Maybe it was seeing a childish person in a sixty-year-old body. But there was more to it than that. There were little surprises in Bill's conversation that were hard to interpret. "What place?" Barry asked.

Bill's face darkened and he shook his head. "I don't want to talk about that place now."

"Talk about what place?"

"Grandville."

"Grandville? Isn't that the state mental institution?"

"Yes, but I'm out now. Ole Bill's out now and I'm doin' fine. And I got me some real hair, like a real good man. I got me a job and I do all the clean-up, and I'm not gonna get in trouble no more."

"Does Harry always treat you that way?" Barry asked. "Yell at you and call you names?"

Bill frowned hard and scrubbed vigorously at the bottom of the pot. "I don't care," he grunted. "I'm not a crackminded old man, so I don't care."

The door swung open and Bev came in. "Barry?" she said and glanced around.

"Hi," Barry answered.

14

"You ready?" She moved to the sink and took Barry's arm. "Hi, Bill."

"Hi," he answered matter-of-factly.

"Well, nice to talk to you, Bill," Barry said.

"Thank you very much," Bill answered. The words came out in a clipped singsong, as if he were mouthing meaningless sounds. "Well, Merry Christmas," he added, then turned sharply. "Hey, Merry Perry!"

"Yeah?" Barry said.

Bill frowned and pointed his scouring pad at Bev. "Is that sweetie your wife?"

Barry smiled. It was one of those surprises again. "Yeah, this sweetie is my wife."

Bill gazed solemnly at the two of them. "You're a lucky guy," he said.

"Thanks, Bill. And Merry Christmas."

Bill appeared to be through talking for the night. He turned back to his pots and pans and resumed scrubbing, rocking gently back and forth.

"Who is that guy?" Barry asked when they reached the car. It was freezing out and Bev sat close to him, waiting for the heater to warm up. At best their little Ford wagon managed to produce a lukewarm gush of air in the winter.

"He came about a month ago," she said. "It's some kind of county program to get mental patients out of institutions and back into the community."

"How bad is he?"

"I don't know. He seems to do the work all right. But he isn't dangerous, or anything. In fact he's very sweet and friendly."

"Where's he live?"

"He has a little room at the club." She laughed. "It's full of hats. Apparently he collects them."

Barry smiled. "Yeah, I saw the one he was wearing tonight."

"No, that's his wig. He's very fond of it. He seems

15

to think that having hair on his head makes him a good man."

"Interesting."

"Why?"

"I don't know. It's just that we tend to think of retarded people as sort of dimwits who don't have any ideas or feelings. I mean we kind of think of them as vegetables. But there seem to be things going on in Bill's head. Like his saying I'm a lucky guy to have a wife like you."

Bev feigned indignance. "I don't think that's so surprising."

"No, seriously. That's sort of a judgmental statement. I mean if he were a vegetable he wouldn't come to any conclusions about good and bad, and lucky and unlucky. You'd just be a woman and I'd be a man. But apparently he's decided you're a good woman, and I'm lucky to have you for a wife. So he's making judgments. And in this case, he happens to be right."

"Thank you very much," she said in Bill's clipped manner.

"That's another thing. Why does he say "Thank you very much" that way? It's almost like a sign-off; like he's ending the conversation with it. When I first walked into the kitchen, the other guy in there was yelling at Bill, telling him to look at the clock. Bill said he didn't like to look at clocks, then cut off the conversation with one of his 'Thank you very much's'."

Bev smiled. "It sounds like as good a way as any to stop someone from yelling at you."

"Yeah, I suppose so. But how come he liked calling me Perry instead of Barry? That kind of suggests a wry sense of humor, doesn't it? I mean it isn't something a vegetable would do. It shows some imagination."

"Maybe he can't pronounce the letter *B*."

"He didn't have any trouble saying his name was Bill." Barry laughed. "William—Bill for short. And I'm Barry, Perry for short."

*　　*　　*

Their apartment was at the top of three flights of stairs, a former loft that had been used to store the business records of a company that had been out of business for fifty years. They had painted it with rich browns and oranges and whites to counter the dinginess, but it was still impossible to keep the place warm in winter.

Shivering from the cold, Barry unlocked the door, stood to the side and smiled as he watched Bev go in. She didn't notice anything unusual at first. She strode immediately to the stove and turned on the burner under the coffee pot. Then she hugged herself for warmth, turned around, and gaped at the kitchen table. "Oh, my God! What's that?!"

It was a big box, all gift-wrapped in silver and white paper with a red ribbon. Barry closed the door and gave the package a puzzled look. "I have no idea. It looks to me like a box."

She glanced suspiciously at him and looked at the card. "'Congratulations,'" she read, "'For the most beautiful mother-to-be in all of Minnesota.'" She stared at him. "Oh, Barry, how did you know?"

"The doctor called here first. Early enough for me to do some shopping."

"You shouldn't have," she said, and tore at the ribbon. "But whatever it is, it's what I've always wanted."

She pulled the top of the carton open and blinked in disbelief. "Carrots?"

Under the bunch of carrots was some celery and a box of tomatoes. "Nothing but the best for you, honey."

"Oh, come on." She dug farther and came to the food processor. "Oh, my God," she gasped.

"It's a juicer. I want the healthiest little mother in Minneapolis."

She pulled it out and stared at it, lifting the top. "It's beautiful. Can we afford it?"

"Well..." Barry shrugged and gathered up the wrapping paper. They couldn't afford it. But they couldn't afford a baby either.

17

"Barry!" she exclaimed, staring at him. "You got the grant!"

He'd sent his best documentary film to the Ford Foundation, and they'd sent an encouraging letter three weeks later saying they had looked at it and found it interesting, and it was going to be reviewed by the awards committee at the next meeting. But the bad news had come three days ago while Bev was at work.

"No," Barry said. "No grant."

She smiled weakly, trying to hide her disappointment. "When did you find out?"

"A couple of days ago. I know I should have told you, honey. But I'm tired of giving you bad news. So here's the good news. The Foundation turned down the film proposal, but they said I could have a job upholstering Fords any time I want. Happy days."

Under the circumstances, it wasn't a very good joke. "A flat rejection?" she asked.

He shrugged. "A lot of nice words that were complimentary. And an offer to look at anything else I had. The usual thing."

"Oh, honey, I'm sorry."

"Yeah, well . . . let's make some juice. Drink a toast to little what's-his-name."

"What's-her-name."

"Let's compromise. What's-it's-name."

Barry was just as happy he hadn't told her about the rejection the day he received it. He had carefully disguised his depression for two days, and had fairly well recovered by the time he passed on the bad news. The world was not exactly coming to an end, and he still had some films out at a couple of universities that conceivably might do him some good. But it still had been a blow; probably because he had gotten his hopes too high after the first letter.

The next morning he slipped out of bed while Bev was still sleeping and made himself coffee. Then he took a deep breath, set up the projector, and took a

typical people. Sort of the statistical mean. And I ended up with three people who were exactly like everybody's neighbor. They were so ordinary there were no surprises. All the people said exactly what you expected them to say. So it was dull, dull, dull. Wonderful lighting and camera work, and beautifully smooth transitions, and all of it so boring it puts you to sleep."

"I didn't think so."

"You're prejudiced. But imagine what it would have been like if I'd had Bill. He's part of the city too. And he's exceptional. He's a guy who could tell us something. Something we don't already know."

"Like what?"

"I don't know. But that's the whole point. A housewife, or a business executive, or a guy who works in a factory—we know exactly what they're thinking about and what they're gonna say. They read the same papers we do, watch the same TV shows, talk about the same things at the dinner table. No surprises. With Bill, who knows what he's thinking about? Who knows what his life has been like? He must be sixty years old, and he's gotten up every day and talked to people and done things every day of those sixty years. And those things are certainly different from what the rest of us have been doing."

Bev stared at him, and Barry suddenly realized his voice was rising with excitement.

"I think it could be fascinating," he said more calmly. "I mean the wig, the night shift at the club, the mental institution. Who put him there in the first place? And why? Did anyone ever try to teach him anything? Does anybody do anything to help him? Has anybody ever even listened to him?"

Bev smiled uncertainly and poured the scrambled eggs into the skillet. "I think I'm witnessing the birth of a new film documentary."

The more Barry thought about it the more he liked the idea. He pulled himself out of the chair and moved to the stove, his hands in his back pockets.

21

"Don't you like the idea? I mean a real down-to-earth, honest picture about what it's like to be a reject in society? Ever since I saw that guy yelling at Bill last night, I haven't been able to get it out of my mind. I mean that guy was talking to Bill as if he were a dog, or something. It was worse than that—nobody would treat a dog that way. But that's how a lot of us tend to think about retarded people: as if they had no feelings...as if they were automatons, or something. But just because he's mentally retarded doesn't mean he doesn't hurt and he doesn't feel lonely and rejected, the same as everybody else. I think it's something worth showing to people; that people like Bill are human. I think it would make a marvelous documentary. Don't you?"

Bev nodded. "I like it. But can we afford it?"

Money suddenly seemed to be no serious problem to Barry. "I could shoot it on video tape. And I could trade off time at the TV station for use of the editing console. I'm sure Carl would go for it. He doesn't have the money to hire me, but he really needs help down there."

Bev knew there was no point in trying to discourage him. It would be like stepping in front of a freight train. "I think it's a great idea," she said. She only hoped it wouldn't take too long. In five or six months it would be a little awkward for her to continue hopping tables at the country club.

III

Carl Amundsen, the manager of the TV station, was not overly impressed with Barry's idea to make a documentary about a sixty-year-old retarded man who washed dishes at a country club. While Barry tried to explain it, Carl answered phone calls, skimmed through sales reports and watched the TV monitors showing the programs of competing stations.

"So what're you gonna do with the thing when you're done?" he finally asked.

Carl was a tall, bony Norwegian who'd spent the last twenty years trying to survive as a small independent TV station surrounded by giants. He lived on coffee, and he'd lost all his hair and half of his stomach from ulcers, and his office was a jungle of stacked film cans and video tapes, old advertising posters, newspapers and dirty coffee cups.

What was he going to do with the project when it was done? Barry hadn't given the question much thought. "I don't know. Maybe sell it to educational TV. Maybe use it as a showcase to get a grant from somebody, or something."

Carl was not impressed with that either. The only thing that ever brightened Carl's day was an idea that might increase his audience share from five percent to seven percent—like a package of *Mary Tyler Moore* reruns at a bargain price.

"Look you wanna come in around four in the afternoon and do some clean-up editing on our library tapes for an hour or two, you can use the equipment all night if you want. Just don't get in anybody's way, okay?"

"Great."

Bill Sackter's room at the country club was behind the kitchen, a windowless little area that probably had been used for storage before he came. When Barry knocked he could hear a television going. The screeching laugh track suggested Bill was watching some situation comedy. The television went off. A moment later Bill answered the door adjusting his haystack wig. He was wearing an old jacket over a sweatshirt.

"Hello, Perry," he said flatly. There was no smile nor any look of curiosity as he glanced at the TV camera Barry was carrying.

"You mind if I come in, Bill? I'd like to talk to you about something."

23

Bill nodded and stepped aside. "Come in. We'll talk about something."

A small neatly made bed stood against the far wall. Across from it a black and white TV set was perched precariously on an ancient dresser. On the wall between them a dozen or more hats were hanging on scattered nails. There were cowboy hats, mashed felts, a fireman's hat, and several billed caps with company names on them. A captain's chair, like those in the coffee shop, was standing in the corner. Bill closed the door and stood silently, waiting.

"Mind if I sit down, Bill?"

"Okay."

"Why don't you sit down, too?"

"Okay. Thank you very much." The old man moved to the bed and sat down. He patted the top of his head, making sure the wig was in place, then gazed blankly at Barry, waiting.

Barry explained what he had in mind; that he wanted to ask Bill some questions and record all of Bill's answers on video tape. And maybe he would take some pictures of Bill at work, and at some other places around town. He would take maybe twenty or thirty hours of pictures, and then edit it down to an hour and a half or so. Would Bill like to do it?

Bill stared at him. "Like a movie?" he asked.

"Yes, like a movie. With you as the star."

Bill nodded thoughtfully. "That's a good idea, Perry," he said.

So far so good. Barry set about adjusting the tripod under the camera, wondering if Bill had any idea of how much work was involved. "What shall we call this movie, Bill?"

Bill had a quick answer. "*I Dream of Jeanie* is a good name."

Barry smiled. "That's a good name. But it's already been taken. Can you think of another name?"

Bill shook his head and frowned at the camera lens. "No."

"How about *The Bill Show*?"

Bill's eyes brightened. "That's a good name. *The Bill Show.*" He nodded.

Barry peered through the camera, adjusting the focus. "Those all your hats on the wall?"

"Yes, those are all my hats."

"How many do you have?"

Bill hesitated; the question seemed to stump him. "All of those. That's how many." He gestured at the wall. "Lots of them."

A well-worn harmonica was lying under the lamp near the bed. "You play that harmonica?" Barry asked.

Bill picked it up. "Yes. I play it real good."

"Well, maybe we'll use it in the film. Now, I want you to sit real still, Bill, so I can get the camera focused."

Bill lifted the harmonica to his mouth and played, moving his head from side to side. It was impossible to focus the camera. "Bill—"

Barry's tone was harsher than he'd intended. Bill quickly put the harmonica on the bedstand. Like a chastised child, he clasped his hands in his lap and stared hard at the floor.

"We'll play the harmonica later, Bill, okay? Now, can you lift your head and look at the camera?"

Bill kept his eyes fixed rigidly on the floor.

"What's the matter, Bill?"

Still no response.

"Are you okay, Bill? What's the matter?"

Bill peered shyly at him, then glanced at the camera and shook his head. "It's that camera. I don't know how to work it." There was a plaintive note in his voice, as if he were confessing a terribly humiliating truth about himself.

Barry quickly suppressed a smile. "You don't have to do a thing, Bill. The camera's already working, all by itself. All you have to do is sit there and tell me about yourself, and I'm going to sit over here and ask you some questions. Okay?"

Bill gazed dubiously at the camera as Barry moved to the chair. "That's all there is?"

"That's all. Now, are you ready? We'll start with an easy question. How old are you, Bill?"

Apparently the question was not so easy after all. Bill opened his hands and clasped them together again, then smiled playfully. "Thirty-three . . . forty-six . . . fifty-eight . . . I'm a real spring chicken." He grinned broadly, pleased with the answer.

At first Barry thought the old man was being coy about his age. Then he realized that the humor was serving a different purpose. Apparently Bill didn't know how old he was, and he was making a joke to cover his ignorance. Barry decided to drop the question. "What do you do at the Minikahda Club?"

Bill suddenly had other things on his mind. "What's this picture gonna be on?" he asked.

"We have to make it first, Bill. Now, what do you do at the Minikahda Club?"

Bill stared fixedly at the camera lens. "Is it gonna be like the *Dream of Jeanie* show? That's a good one."

Barry took a long, fortifying breath. He'd told Bill he would shoot twenty or thirty hours of tape. It looked like it was going to be more like fifty or sixty at the rate they were going. "I'll do my best, Bill. Now, you want to tell me what you do at the Minikahda Club?"

It took twenty minutes to get Bill's description of his work in the kitchen. His mind seemed to fix on one subject, and there was no getting him back to the point until he grew bored with it. He talked about the *Jeanie* show for a while, and then repeated his story about the man who had beat him up the previous night. When he got around to his duties in the kitchen he said he cleaned pots and pans and dishes and knives and forks and plates, and more pots and pans.

He had been collecting hats for a long time, he said. He collected hats before he had his wig, and he always wore a hat before he got his wig. But it was better to have a wig because it was like real hair, and having real hair made him a "good" man. Did Barry want him to play the harmonica now?

"No," Barry said, he wanted Bill to talk.

Bill was still suspicious of the camera. Apparently it made no sense to him that the camera could be making pictures by just standing there on its tripod.

"Okay," Barry said. "So, before the Minikahda Club, you were in the State Mental Institution at Grandville, right, Bill?"

The question dampened Bill's spirits considerably. "Yes, I was at Grandville," he mumbled.

"And how long were you there?"

Bill shook his head as if trying to shake off the question. "Too long, buddy," he said with a touch of bitterness. "I was there many years. I was there too long; so long I didn't know I was there."

"And why did they put you there to begin with?"

Bill fidgeted and pushed his lower lip in and out. "Said I was a crackminded man," he mumbled. "I couldn't handle my systems. I was a low-grade man."

"Is that true?"

"Noooo," he protested. "I could handle my systems."

"Fine," Barry said. He moved to the camera and carefully adjusted the lens to a tight close-up on Bill. Through the eyepiece he could see Bill's face darken.

"What are you doing?" Bill asked.

Barry didn't want to get into a protracted discussion about the camera again. "Close-up," he said, and quickly went on: "So, tell me some more about Grandville, Bill."

It was obviously a painful subject. Bill shook his head. He looked at his hats, then at the door, then at his harmonica.

"Come on, Bill."

"No," Bill said petulantly.

"Why not?"

"It's a hellhole," he grumbled.

The Bill Show," Barry reminded him. It was the key

phrase that had gotten Bill back on the track twice before. This time it had no magical effect.

"No," Bill said again. "It's a hellhole."

"Bill—"

"I don't want to talk about that. No. No. No. No."

"Come on, Bill. We're making a movie here."

"I don't want to talk about that no more."

This time he spoke with an airy finality that suggested he'd put it out of his mind for the rest of the day, and nothing was going to bring it back.

"Why not?" Barry asked.

"I don't want to talk about it no more." He suddenly picked up his harmonica and played, blowing a spirited rendition of "Danny Boy."

"Come on, Bill," Barry pleaded.

"No," Bill said between breaths, and continued playing.

Barry eased back in the chair and watched as Bill happily lost himself in the music. It was another one of Bill's surprises. As easygoing as he appeared to be, apparently there were some borderlines you didn't cross, and Grandville was one of them. It was obviously too painful for him to think about, and he simply dropped an iron curtain to protect himself from that pain.

Barry let the camera run, realizing he was going to have a big editing job when he finished battling with all of Bill's mood changes. In spite of all the digressions, however, he was pleased with the way things were going. There was no way to anticipate how a person might behave in front of a camera. The world's greatest extroverts often froze into catatonic bundles of fear and anxiety, and the most taciturn and laconic people imaginable sometimes became all-star performers. But Bill—maybe because he had few complex layers of pride and inhibitions—hardly seemed aware of the camera once he got rolling.

"How about some lunch?" Barry asked when Bill finished the tune.

"Sure," Bill said and jumped to his feet. "Thank you very much."

After Barry went home that afternoon, Bill didn't turn on the TV again. Instead he stretched out on the bed, folded his hands on his chest and smiled happily at the ceiling. He liked Barry-Perry Morrow, and he liked talking to him and making *The Bill Show*.

It had been a long time since he had talked so much and anybody had listened to him. When he was in Grandville a man named Dr. Weir had asked him questions and listened to him talk sometimes two or three days a week. But Dr. Weir had gone somewhere else—to Chicago, somebody had told him—and then there wasn't anybody who wanted to talk to him much anymore.

Since he'd gotten out of Grandville he'd had lots of jobs, but nobody ever talked to him much, or wanted to know anything about him. He was just a crackminded old man, and sometimes people shouted at him as if he couldn't hear good. Or they laughed, or said things about him when they thought he wasn't listening.

Bill smiled and nodded to himself and played his harmonica for a while. He hoped they never finished *The Bill Show*, and that he and Barry-Perry just kept on talking and being buddies.

A mild disaster occurred in the following week. Rather than continue questioning Bill in his room, Barry decided to break the monotony with some outdoor action footage. As important as it was to hear what Bill had to say, he also wanted to see him functioning in ordinary situations that normal people handled without thinking.

To start with, some simple task seemed appropriate; something that would not tax Bill too much, and would give Barry an idea of just how far he could go with this sort of thing. So he drove Bill toward town, and then parked the car in a residential district close to a fairly busy intersection.

At the corner, four or five people were bundled up against the cold, waiting for a bus.

"Have you ever ridden on a public bus?" he asked Bill.

"I don't know," he said. He seemed indifferent to the question, neither frightened by the idea, nor eager to try it.

Barry was as interested to see how he would interact with the other people as he was to see Bill on the bus. "Okay, I'm going to give you fifty cents, and I want you to go wait with those people on the corner. A bus will come along any minute now, and I want you to get on with those people and give the money to the bus driver. Okay?"

Bill took a minute to absorb all the instructions. "Okay," he said.

Barry got the camera from the back seat and gave Bill the money. "Now I'm going to take your picture doing all that, so I don't want you to look at me. Okay?"

"For *The Bill Show*," Bill said.

"Right, for *The Bill Show*."

"That's good, Perry. I'll get on the bus." Bill pushed open the door and they both got out.

"You got your money ready?"

Bill nodded as they walked toward the corner. "Thank you very much."

"All right, you just keep going, and don't look back. I'm going to shoot the picture from here."

Bill kept walking, shuffling along, swaying a little from side to side. He almost looked like a circus clown. Barry smiled and focused the camera, following him all the way to the group of people. Keeping his face studiously turned away from the camera, Bill stopped beside a heavy woman holding a bag of groceries. He smiled at her and woman moved closer to the curb, glancing suspiciously back at him. It was exactly the kind of thing Barry wanted.

Barry moved closer along the curb and resumed shooting. He could now see all of the faces except that of his principal actor. After a quick glance back, Bill turned his head, looking in the opposite direction.

The bus suddenly came roaring in behind Barry, the brakes hissing and squealing and the diesel engine rattling as it rolled to a stop. The front door opened and the people filed on board, Bill bringing up the rear. With the two quarters held out in front of him, he stepped up through the doors and disappeared. No problems so far; Bill had handled the situation like an old pro.

Barry quit shooting and strode toward the front of the bus. But he had taken no more than three steps when the brakes suddenly hissed, the engine roared and spewed out diesel smoke, and the bus was moving.

"Hey, hold it!" Barry shouted. He broke into a run and waved his free arm at the driver's mirror. "Stop the bus! Hold it! Stop! Stop!"

The big machine continued gathering speed through the intersection. Then it was rumbling down the street, lost in a sea of traffic.

My God, what had he done? Barry stared, dumbfounded as the bus grew smaller and smaller. Would Bill panic when he realized he was alone? Would he get off the bus at the next stop? Or would he ride all the way to the end of the line? Barry raced back to the car, suddenly feeling like an idiot. How could he have done such a stupid thing?

The bus driver must have been behind schedule and racing to catch up. When Barry reached the next bus stop, the bus was nowhere in sight. Nor was Bill standing on the corner.

Same at the next stop.

Finally, five minutes later, Barry caught sight of the bus just as it was pulling away from the curb. He skirted through traffic and edged up beside it, searching the windows.

Bill was seated in the first seat behind the driver.

There was no mistaking him; he was sitting straight, gazing through the front window, his silly wig now tilted slightly forward over his eyes. There was no look of panic or concern on his face; he looked like a bored commuter, half asleep as he waited for the bus to reach his destination. Except Bill didn't have any destination.

Barry honked and leaned forward, peering out the windshield. Bill paid no attention, and he honked again.

Still no response. At least none from Bill. But the drivers of the cars behind him suddenly were becoming unhappy over the traffic lane being blocked. First one and then another honked, drowning out Barry's own horn.

There was nothing else to do. Barry drove on and let the other cars pass. Then he fell in behind the bus and followed it through downtown Minneapolis and four or five miles out into the suburbs.

The bus finally reached the end of the line, and Barry parked behind it and jumped out of the car. Bill was the only passenger left. The driver spoke to him for a minute, then both of them got out. Barry hurried over and grabbed Bill's arm. "You okay?"

Bill didn't seem surprised to see him. "I'm fine, thank you very much. Did I do everything right?"

Barry let out a sigh and walked him back to the car. "You did fine. Didn't you hear me honking next to the bus?"

"No," Bill said. "I was talking to the bus driver. His name is Robert, Bob for short."

"Get in the car, Bill."

Bill slid in and Barry got back behind the wheel. "What time do you have to be at work?"

Bill wasn't concerned about it; he was too pleased with his accomplishments. "I don't know."

"Don't you have regular hours?"

The question seemed to puzzle him. But as he did with most things that puzzled him, he ignored the question. He turned away and looked out the window. "These are pretty houses."

Barry drove in silence back to the country club. "Listen, Bill," he said when they stopped in the parking lot. "Sooner or later we're going to have to talk about Grandville. I know it upsets you, but it's an important part of *The Bill Show.*"

Barry saw the hands come together and the jaw tighten. Bill stared out the side window. Then his thoughts drifted off to something else. His hands relaxed and he hummed softly to himself.

"Well, I think that's enough for today, Bill. And I imagine you've got to go to work."

Bill smiled and pushed the door open. "Thank you very much," he said.

IV

Through the next week Bill talked about the other places he had worked. From what Barry could gather, he'd had four or five jobs in the past two years, most of them working in kitchens. He'd also been a janitor and general clean-up man in a lumber yard, and he talked about being "pinched" by the police and being beaten up a number of times.

A name that cropped up frequently was Miss Keating, a "nice brown-skinned" lady who helped Bill get jobs and get him out of jail. Barry guessed the woman was a social worker of some sort, and he made a note to talk to her.

After the first week, Bill was always waiting for him in the parking lot. "Just standing out here waiting for my buddy," he'd say with a big smile.

He still balked at any mention of Grandville, and Barry made only indirect references to it. Was the food at the country club better than at Grandville? Did you have a room like this at Grandville, Bill?

Sometimes he answered, and sometimes he said he

didn't want to talk about the place. But as the days passed his reactions to the name seemed to be less severe.

After the sessions every day, Barry went over to the TV station and worked two or three hours going through the old library tapes, editing and cataloguing them. Then he ran his own tapes, timing them and making a detailed description of all the material.

He still didn't know what he was going to do with the material. There was no question about Bill being a colorful character, and that there were all kinds of things going on in his head. The missing ingredient, however, was any kind of cohesive background that might provide some perspective on Bill's present situation.

Barry was mulling over this problem one night as he trudged up the stairs and pushed open the door to the apartment. Bev was sitting at the kitchen table with a cup of coffee and a book. Her cleaned dinner plate was on the kitchen sink, and the look she gave him was not exactly warm.

"Hi," he said, realizing he hadn't left the TV station until after nine o'clock.

"Hi, Barry," she answered. Her tone was about two degrees lower than the temperature outside.

He put the TV camera on the couch and gave her a beaming smile. "Hey, I'm sorry I'm late. How was your day?"

She didn't lift her head, so he gave her a kiss on the ear. The book that was occupying her attention was called *Childbirth Without Pain.*

"Terrific," she said. "You're dinner's in the oven. It's been drying to a pleasant hardness."

"Great. Just the way I like it. Mmmm. I'm hungry."

The food in the oven looked like meatloaf with potatoes and carrots. But he couldn't be certain. Maybe it was a lump of coal. He scraped it out with a spatula and dropped it on a plate.

"Where've you been?" she asked. "You know, Barry,

it's been three nights now. One, two, three. I've hardly seen you all week."

So that was the problem—his nightly disappearing act. "I know, and I'm really sorry, honey. I really am. And I'll be here tomorrow and tomorrow and tomorrow and tomorrow. One, two, three, four. Okay?" He smiled happily at her, challenging her to respond.

She tried to hold the gloomy face, but it finally cracked. "Okay," she laughed. "But I do enjoy your company now and then. That's one of the reasons I agreed to be your wife."

"And you made a very smart decision. And I promise to love, honor and behave, and hang around a lot more."

"Okay," she said. She leaned across and gave him a kiss.

Peace was restored.

Barry scraped the crust from the meatloaf and dug in. "It's just that this thing's going so good that I forget the time," he said. "Going a lot better than I thought it would. Bill was shy at first, and we had some rough days. But he's really starting to come out of himself now. He hasn't got the subtleties of an adult mind, but he's got this innocence...this basic honesty that's like a child. That's what's coming through. I thought it was going to be depressing, but he's really funny sometimes. Going over the tapes, it's just fun to watch him. It's refreshing."

"It sounds good," she said.

"Yeah. Except there's one little problem. He won't talk about Grandville."

"I don't think I would either if I were he."

"No. But I've got to have it on film. I mean that's the incredible part of it; that he's not broken and bitter over the whole experience. The audience has to know what kind of place Grandville was before they can appreciate what Bill's life has been. You can say Auschwitz was a terrible place, but that doesn't mean much to anybody unless you can show them how really bad it was."

"I suppose so," she said.

"I'd like to take him out there Monday. I'd like to get some pictures of the place, and get his reaction to it."

"You think he'll go?"

"Probably not. Not without some darned good reason. And Bill's darned good reasons are different from everybody else's. You could offer him a million dollars to do something, and it wouldn't mean a thing to him."

Bev got up and brought him a piece of pie from the refrigerator. "He likes you, doesn't he?"

"I think he likes me very much. I'm the only friend he's got. I'm his "buddy." But when I mention Grandville, he picks up his harmonica and disappears from the world. So should I trade our friendship for pictures of Grandville?"

Bev shook her head. "I don't know," she said quietly.

Barry wished she had been more decisive. He knew he had to take Bill out there, and the decision would be easier with some strong moral support.

It snowed most of Sunday night. On Monday morning, the sky was clear, but the temperature was close to zero and the streets were solid ice. Barry was forty-five minutes late getting to the country club, but Bill was in the parking lot, all bundled up in an overcoat and wearing a hunter's cap with earmuffs. He hurried over to the car, smiling apprehensively.

"I thought maybe you weren't coming," he said. "But I waited for you. I waited for you since I ate my breakfast."

"You're a good buddy, Bill. Why don't you get in the car and warm up?"

Bill hurried around and climbed in. "Yup," he said, almost singing. "We're buddies, Perry. That's why

I waited for you." He nodded and rocked in the seat, smiling happily. "What are we gonna do today, Perry?"

"Well...That's what I want to talk to you about, Bill. About our picture."

"The Bill Show."

"Right. *The Bill Show.* And we want it to be a good picture. We want it to be as good as *Jeanie,* don't we?"

"As good as *Jeanie.* Yes, that's a good one."

"And sometimes Jeanie does things she doesn't want to do, doesn't she? Things that are not always pleasant for her. Right?"

Bill gazed at him and nodded, but a shadow of doubt clouded his eyes. He didn't understand.

Barry sighed and watched an elderly couple make their way gingerly across the icy parking lot and up to the clubhouse. "Let me put it this way, Bill. To make *The Bill Show* good, we've got to show people what your life has been like, right? I mean we've got to show more than your room, and what you do here at the country club. We've got to show what things were like for you in the past."

"Okay," Bill agreed.

Good old agreeable Bill—he had no idea what was coming. "Look, Bill, an important part of your past...and a very important thing for *The Bill Show* is Grandville."

Bill gazed steadily at him until the dreaded word was spoken. Then he turned quickly and stared out the windshield. The only good sign was that he didn't reach for his harmonica.

"I know it's tough for you, Bill. But I want to go out there today. I want to take pictures of the place. And I want you to go with me."

"I don't wanna go there," he said quietly.

Barry took a deep breath. It was unfair, but he didn't know of any other way. "Do you want me to quit making *The Bill Show*?"

Bill's jaw quivered and he blinked several times, still staring through the windshield. He finally swallowed and shook his head. "No," he said.

"I know it's very hard, Bill. But I think you can do it. And I'm not going to let anything happen to you. I'm your buddy, right?"

Bill lowered his head and nodded. "You're my buddy," he said almost inaudibly.

"Do you trust me?"

"Yes, I trust you," he whispered.

Barry started the car. "Okay, we're going to drive out there, and in two or three hours we're going to be right back here at the country club. Both of us. We're going to stick together. Right, buddy?"

"All right," Bill answered. "You're my buddy. We're going to stick together."

Barry smiled and swung the car around. "Buddies all the way."

Grandville was only forty-five minutes away, but it was probably the longest drive Bill ever took in his life. As if trying to take his mind off the situation and bolster his spirits, he played his harmonica for a while. Then he put it away, hunched his shoulders, and stared through the windshield as if expecting his deadliest enemy to loom up before him at any minute. The old ghosts were stirring, and he was doing everything he could to keep them at bay.

Grandville was a huge brick building. A chain-link fence surrounded the grounds, and the trees were stark black skeletons against the fresh snow. All of the windows in the building were secured with heavy steel grating, and many had window shades that appeared to be torn and sagging.

Maybe the place looked better in the summertime when the trees had leaves. But now all it needed was a stormy night and some hounds baying in the woods behind it.

The gate was open, suggesting there were no serious security problems. Or maybe it was too cold for anyone to attempt an escape. Barry had already talked to the director of the institution—a man named Peters, who had voiced no objections to Barry bringing Bill back for a visit. He had sounded like a friendly, intelligent man, and he'd been pleased to hear Bill was getting along all right on the outside.

Either Bill had reconciled himself to the visit to his old prison, or he had become paralyzed into silence by the prospect. He sat stiffly in the seat and stared at the building as if mesmerized by the memories it brought back. Barry parked the car and got his eight millimeter camera from the back seat. "You okay, Bill?"

Bill nodded stiffly, and Barry pushed open his door. "Stay in the car for a minute. I want to get a picture of you getting out, with the building in the background."

Bill nodded and Barry moved around to a position behind the car. "Okay," he shouted.

Bill opened the door and slowly got out. He gave Barry a glance, then turned quickly back toward the building, as if alert for any sudden attack from the rear.

"Okay, walk over to the front door."

Bill fidgeted, looking from Barry to the building. Then he shuffled past the car and walked halfway to the steps. He stopped and looked back. "Aren't you coming?" he asked uneasily.

He was probably torn with doubts and fears: Was he being tricked into returning to the place? Was Barry really his buddy? Barry couldn't put any more pressure on him. He quit filming and strode forward. "I'm coming, buddy."

The reception room had a threadbare carpet and an old oak desk that looked as if it had been discarded by the local school district. The woman behind it took their names, and two minutes later Dr. Peters materialized through a door. He was a portly man in his sixties with white hair and weary, smiling eyes.

"Hello, Bill," he said after he shook Barry's hand. "You're looking fine."

Bill shook the man's hand, but he couldn't bring himself to speak. He fidgeted nervously and glanced around the room as if expecting it to close in on him.

"Let's go to the file room, Mr. Morrow," Peters said. "And Bill, maybe you'd like to visit with some of your old friends."

Bill nodded, still too nervous to speak.

The interior corridors didn't look any better than the reception room. They followed the doctor down a long hallway, and he finally opened a heavy door. Barry smiled at Bill. "Why don't you wait in there, Bill. Mr. Morrow and I will be just across the hall in the file room."

Bill glanced in the room, then stared uneasily at the doctor.

"We won't be long," Barry said reassuringly.

The doctor smiled again and pointed into the room. "Bill, I think you know someone in there."

The statement piqued bill's curiosity enough that he peered inside. Then his tension suddenly dissolved and he moved through the door.

"Hi, buddy," he said, suddenly smiling happily.

The man inside looked as if he was in his sixties and suffering from malnutrition. He was hunched forward in a wheelchair, his mouth drooping and his eyes glazed and expressionless. He stared vacantly at Bill and watched him sit down.

"It's me," Bill said cheerfully. "Wild Bill from Borneo. How you been, Ray?"

Ray stared dully at him and said nothing.

"I got me a buddy, Ray. Got me a buddy. Yes sirree, and he's makin' a movie show, a real movie show, and I'm in that show. Just like downtown."

The man blinked indifferently. Then he lifted his hand and moved it back and forth across his mouth.

Bill knew exactly what the man was trying to communicate. He pulled his harmonica from his coat pocket. "You want me to play a song? All right, all right, I'll play you one, then."

The man stared blankly at him as Bill tried a couple of notes then played "My Old Kentucky Home."

Dr. Peters smiled at Barry and they moved across the hall. "Everybody here likes Bill's music. They've missed him."

"I don't think Bill misses this place much," Barry answered.

Dr. Peters pulled out a file cabinet drawer and searched through a mass of dog-eared folders. "No, I don't suppose he does. Grandville was built in 1910. At the time it was considered a model institution. Unfortunately its time of service seems to have passed. Most of the wards are empty now."

"What happened to everyone?"

"Community placement. It was a very popular program in the late sixties. Most of the patients were placed in and around Minneapolis."

The building seemed exceptionally quiet. Occasionally a wheelchair rolled past the open door of the file room, but there were no screams or thumps from head-banging.

"Ahh, here we are," Peters said and pulled out a manila folder. They both moved to a table and sat down.

"Bill Sackter," Peters said, reading from a sheaf of records. "Diagnosis: Mental deficiency...imbecilic...cause undiagnosed. He was here for forty-six years."

"Forty-six years?" That was half again as long as Barry had lived.

Peters nodded. "He was just a boy when he arrived. Seven years old. His mother committed him to the institution."

Barry shook his head in disbelief. "His mother took a seven-year-old child and put him in a place like this to rot for forty-four years? What kind of a family did he have?"

Peters shrugged and shuffled through the papers. "We don't have a lot of information on patients this old. Apparently his father was deceased ... his mother was poor. She didn't know how to handle him. They were

41

immigrants. She never communicated with Bill after he came to Grandville."

Barry couldn't understand it. "Why was he kept here so long? He's able to get around fine."

Peters closed the folder and sat back. "That's true. But the laws and attitudes were different in those days. He was just like thousands of others with subnormal intelligence and severe learning disabilities. I don't think Bill ever scored higher than a five- or six-year-level."

"How could he?" Barry said. "He didn't have a chance being kept here all the time."

Peters nodded. "I'm afraid you're right. Mr. Morrow, sometimes a patient can get lost in a place like this—especially if his family doesn't care. There's never been enough money to give individual attention to people like Bill. We all seem to feel there are more important things to do with our tax money."

There was a faint note of bitterness in his voice, and Barry couldn't blame him. "What about his family? Where are they?"

"Deceased," Peters said. "Except for a sister named Sarah."

"Where is she?"

"I don't know. It's not in the records."

Barry wondered if Bill knew about his sister. Or if he ever thought about the mother who had abandoned him. "If people like Bill are able to get out of this place," he said, "what kind of patients do you have left?"

"Very severe cases. Patients who are totally dependent; the ones who couldn't be placed."

"Is it possible to see any of them?"

Peters hesitated, then pulled himself up. "Yes, I can show you one of the wards downstairs."

As they walked out of the file room Barry paused and looked through the open door to check on Bill. He was still sitting with his friend, Ray. The man had some kind of a board with pegs resting on his lap. He picked up one of the pegs and threw it across the room, then cackled with delight.

"Don't do that," Bill said.

The man cackled and pulled out another peg.

"Don't do those things," Bill said firmly. "Ray, people won't like you if you throw those things. You want me to play you another song?"

Ray stopped cackling and stared as Bill played the harmonica again. Barry listened for a minute, then followed the doctor toward the staircase.

"Have you ever been in a mental ward before, Mr. Morrow?" Peters asked as they went down the stairs.

The lower corridors were like tombs in an old prison. "No," Barry said.

Peters paused before opening the door. "Just be quiet and stand in the back of the room. If it bothers you, let me know and we'll leave."

It was a large room with padded benches and chairs. About a dozen men were scattered around. Some of them were lying on the floor, curled into fetal positions. Others were staring off at nothing, their mouths hanging open. A man who appeared to be in his twenties was on his hands and knees, methodically banging his head on the floor—his skull protected with a football helmet. Others were drooling, or making strangled noises as if trying to speak. The smell of human waste was overpowering.

Most of the patients paid no attention to the visitors. They were in a world of their own, totally oblivious to their surroundings. A skinny old man with a misshapen head shuffled over to Dr. Peters and grabbed the doctor's arm with both hands, making sounds like an infant child.

"Hello, Bobby," Peters said quietly. The man released his grip and stroked the doctor's arm, then shuffled off. In the corner of the room he put his hands on the wall and laughed hysterically.

It was in here that Bill had spent forty-six years of his life. It was incredible that he was able to function at all. While other children were going to movies and learning how to play baseball, Bill had been surrounded by crippled minds and tortured bodies, men who couldn't even control their own bodily functions. What a shock it must have been for him to come out into a world of normal people. To Bill, normality had been grunting, slobbering men who stared at walls and made no effort to communicate with each other.

"I think I've seen enough," Barry said. He was beginning to feel nauseated.

Peters nodded and led the way out, then carefully locked the door behind him. "There's very little we can do for them," he said as they returned to the stairs. "Keep them alive, and protect them from themselves and each other. There are some even worse than those; men who have to be kept under constant restraint, or under heavy sedation."

"Could I come back some time and take pictures?" Barry asked. He wasn't sure he really wanted to.

"Yes. Just let me know ahead of time. Anything else you'd like to see?"

"No, thanks. I think that's plenty for one day. And I'd better get back to Bill."

The doctor stopped at the intersection of two corridors. "Fine. Then I'll be getting back to my office. Nice to meet you, Mr. Morrow."

"You too, doctor." Barry shook his hand and walked back toward the file room, breathing deeply to calm his stomach.

The door to Ray's room was still open, but Barry could hear no harmonica music. He turned the corner into the room, then stopped short.

Ray was still sitting in his wheelchair, the pegboard still resting on his lap. But Bill was nowhere in sight. "Where's Bill?" he asked.

Ray didn't look up. His hands moved jerkily across the pegboard as if trying to find a peg, but there was no indication that he'd heard the question. "Oh, my God!" Barry said and quickly returned to the corridor.

Had Bill wandered off to see more of his friends? Or had he crossed the corridor to the file room, and panicked when he found it empty? "Bill!" Barry shouted.

He walked toward the far end of the corridor, then broke into a run. "Bill!!"

The staircase going up was blocked by heavy doors. He must have gone down. "Bill!!" Barry took the steps three at a time. Another possibility loomed into Barry's mind—a guard, maybe a new man who didn't know the patients well, might have mistaken Bill for one of the inmates.

At the bottom of the stairs, Barry paused indecisively. Corridors ran off in three directions. "Bill!"

Then he heard it; a distant, muffled cry of desperation. "Barry!"

Where had it come from? Barry listened for a minute, then ran down the middle corridor. "Bill? Where are you?"

"Barrryyyyy!" The cry was full of despair, like that of a drowning man using his last ounce of breath.

Barry skidded to a stop at an intersection and looked in both directions. Then he spotted him. Bill was crossing the corridor from side to side wildly trying to open locked doors. "Barrrryyyy!" he whimpered helplessly.

"Bill, I'm here!"

The old man whirled, trembling, gaping at him like a cornered animal. Then he hurried forward, still panicked, glancing at the doors on either side as if fearing somebody might jump out and grab him.

Barry gave him a reassuring smile. "You thought I'd left you, didn't you? I wouldn't do that. You okay?"

Bill managed a weak smile and nodded, catching his breath. "You weren't in the other room where you said you'd be," he said in a suddenly childish voice. "You were gone."

Barry put an arm around his shoulders and they walked toward the stairs. "I left for just a couple minutes, buddy. When I came back you were gone. You ready to leave this place?"

Bill nodded vigorously. "I'm ready to leave."

When he was safely back in the car Bill rocked gently back and forth and gazed out at the building as if it were a raging inferno from which he had just escaped.

Barry started the engine and waited for the heater to warm up. "I'm sorry, Bill. Maybe I shouldn't have taken you back there."

"It's all right, buddy. I'm all right now." He repeated the statement as if trying to convince himself that he was finally safe.

"Where was your family all the time you were in there, Bill?"

Bill ignored the question and continued rocking.

"Dr. Peters said you have a sister. Is that true?"

"I have a sister. Her name is Sarah."

"Is that your only family?"

"I don't like to talk about it," Bill said. He reached up to pat his wig, but it was covered by the hat. He sighed heavily and seemed to be recovering now.

"Do you have a wallet?" Barry asked.

He nodded. "I have a wallet. I have a good wallet."

"Pictures of your family? I.D.?"

Bill searched the pockets of his coat, then his pants. He found the wallet and handed it over, smiling, pleased with his success. "Here's my wallet."

There were scraps of paper, pictures torn from magazines and newspapers, some rubber bands. "What's this?"

Bill squinted at it. "That's my card."

"Your welfare card?"

"Uh-huh. It says I belong to Miz Keating."

"She's your welfare officer, right?"

"Yes." He nodded as if pleased that everything was understood now.

"What's this?" It was a piece of paper money

folded four or five times and stuffed deeply into one of the pockets. Barry unfolded it.

"That's my regular good luck piece," Bill said gravely. "It's my two-dollar bill." He peered over at it and nodded. "There's a picture of Thomas Jefferson. He's a real good man. Born April thirteenth, just like old Bill."

Barry smiled and returned the bill to its hiding place. "Feels pretty lucky to me." He handed back the wallet and put the car in gear. "Shall we get out of here?"

"Okay, buddy," Bill said. "Let's get out of here."

V

Bill was becoming a real celebrity around the television station. Barry had brought him in two or three times to tape interview sessions when there were unoccupied sound booths. Some of the employees had been curious, and then they'd wandered in to watch the sessions.

The biggest crowd came the night Barry recorded Bill singing and playing his harmonica. Bill loved having an audience, and there was more than a little ham in him. He sat on a straight-backed chair and made sure his black haystack was squarely on top of his head and then looked gravely at the camera as if he were the King of England sitting for a portrait.

"Okay, Bill, beautiful," Barry said and adjusted a microphone in front of him. "You know what this is?"

Bill gave a single nod. "It's a microphone."

"It's a microphone. Right. Mike for short."

"Mike for short. William, Bill for short. Microphone, Mike for short. Barry, Perry for short."

The five or six people outside the glass all grinned. "Mike for short," Bill said again, enjoying the response.

"Right," Barry said and picked up his guitar. "Now,

I'm going to play a little bit, and when I nod like this you come in. Okay?"

Barry played an eight bar introduction to "Billy Boy," and nodded. Bill took a deep breath and sang, his voice hoarse and slightly off-key, but full of drama and enthusiasm.

> Oh, where have you been, Billy Boy, Billy Boy.
> Where have you been darling Bill?
> I've been down to the farm, didn't do no harm...
> You can make a cherry pie, darling Bill."

Bill grabbed his harmonica and joined the guitar for the second verse. Barry picked up the tempo and Bill kept up with him and added a few imaginative riffs of his own. They were really swinging by the end. Bill finished it with a long and loud: *"You can make a cherry pie, d-a-a-a-r-r-r-l-i-i-i-n-n-n-g Billy!"*

The spectators clapped and cheered, and Barry laughed happily. "Wow—Wild Bill!!" he exclaimed.

"Billy Boy," Bill said and nodded. "That was pretty good."

"It's a million dollar hit," Barry agreed.

Other nights were long sessions in which Bill told about the miseries of Grandville. There were beatings and general neglect. He told of a young boy being thrown down the stairs when he was having what sounded like an epileptic seizure. When Bill tried to get help for the boy, one of the attendants kicked him so hard in the stomach he had to have two operations.

Bill continued to say he didn't want to talk about Grandville. But it was now more of a rote protest that he tossed off and then ignored. Barry suspected that their visit to the place had done Bill far more good than harm.

Over the following months, the films and tapes were piling up and Bill was having a wonderful time telling his tales and recording his music. Barry also had to admit he was enjoying the project.

It was a happy collaboration, and for the first time in his short career as a filmmaker, Barry was certain the material was good. It was better than good. It was different, fresh and insightful, and his principal actor was growing more charming every day.

And then, in early June, while in the baby department of a downtown department store, reality brought the whole project to an abrupt halt. Barry was following Bev through the racks of baby clothes and the shelves full of dolls and teddy bears, thinking about Bill and how Bill had been complaining about his false teeth lately, when it happened.

Bev was wearing maternity clothes now, the baby the size of a basketball under her smock. She was walking slowly when she reached the display of cribs. There were pink ones and blue ones and white ones, all decorated with little flowers and circus animals. Bev gave them all an assessing glance, then bent over and peered at the price tag on the closest one.

"How much?" Barry asked.

She smiled wanly and moved on to the next one. "One hundred and ten dollars and eighty-nine cents."

What happened to the good old days when you put the baby in a dresser drawer, Barry wondered. "My Mom might have some of that stuff around." He gave her a shrugging smile. "Of course it's kind of old. Don't fit me anymore."

Bev wasn't amused. "I want new things for the baby. Not hand-me-downs." She moved on to the next crib.

"The stuff is in good shape," Barry said. "I didn't use it much. Besides, babies don't need a place to sleep. They cry all night."

Bev was not in a smiling mood today, and Barry felt what was coming. It had been building slowly through the past couple of months; every time she mentioned the high cost of food, the utility bills, and the cost of gas and insurance for the car. He could only dismiss those things with jokes so long, and no matter how

49

much he talked about how wonderful the project with Bill was coming along, it was still bringing in no cash.

"Barry," she said, and looked at him across a yellow crib, "the hospital bill's going to be a thousand dollars."

"I know," he said. "We'll figure it out."

"A thousand dollars," she repeated. "We don't have it."

"I'll get it," he said. "I've been looking for a job, and I'll get it." The statement was only partially true. The other day he had asked Carl Amundsen if he knew of any openings at the other TV stations, but Carl had not been encouraging.

"How?" she asked. "All you've been doing is working on *The Bill Show.*"

Barry nodded. "But it's really special, Bev," he said weakly. "I can feel it. It's going to be good."

"Barry, you're living in a dream world," she sighed. "You apply for film grants and nothing ever comes through. You teach filmmaking to glue-sniffing teenagers and you get the tires slashed on the car. You know, the last time I counted, you had four jobs; aspiring screenwriter, aspiring novelist, aspiring rock musician, and "in-between" filmmaker. None of them pays the rent."

It was ridiculous to be having a conversation like this in a department store. A grandmotherly saleswoman had started toward them, but then veered discreetly away. The other shoppers were also giving them a wide berth. "We get by," he said quietly.

"Because I work as a waitress. But I'm not going to be working at the club much longer. Time's running out now. We're going to have to get it together. Soon."

"Okay, honey," he said and moved toward the furniture department. She joined him, her eyes suddenly moist.

"Babies don't wait for film grants, Barry. They don't wait for you to get your life together, to be a success." She caught her breath for a moment and put her hand on her stomach.

"You okay?"

She nodded, then sat down on a shiny sofa with a thousand dollar price tag. Barry sat down beside her and took her hand. Tears were skidding down her cheeks. "I just get so scared for us...for the future," she said. "I mean, an unfinished film...no job...baby on the way...it's like a bad dream."

"Hey, hey, come on," he said.

"You're going to have to forget the film...at least for a while. I can't do it anymore alone. Promise me, Barry, please."

Barry took a deep breath and let it out slowly. She was right; he was living in a dream world. His total earning from teaching and doing odd jobs in the past three years had been less than seven thousand dollars. And even if *The Bill Show* was a smash success, it could be years before he got any money from it. It was time for him to enter the real world.

"Okay," he said, "I promise. No more film for a while. I'll just get a regular job till something comes along."

"Really?" she said doubtfully.

"Really. I promise." He put his arm around her shoulders and grinned. "Now give me one of those big smiles of yours, okay?"

The tears had stopped. She found a handkerchief and dabbed at her nose, managing a smile. "Thank you," she said.

The full impact of what he had promised didn't hit him until late that night when Bev was curled up and sleeping peacefully with her head on his shoulder. To celebrate the great job-hunting decision he had taken her to their favorite Italian restaurant and they had eaten all the spaghetti five dollars would buy. Then they had come home and made love, and for the first time in months Bev had seemed totally relaxed and optimistic about the future. Five minutes later she was asleep, breathing deeply, her arm loosely across his chest. Barry gazed thoughtfully into the darkness.

He was not overly concerned about finding a job. If necessary he would wash windows, or paint houses, or do gardening work. But what would Bill do? For the past four or five months, Bill's entire life had been wrapped around doing *The Bill Show.* They'd spent almost every day together, and for Bill it was like a small child going to Disneyland day after day. Bill had found a "buddy," and it was the biggest thing in his life.

So what could he tell him? How could he explain to Bill that life was not all singing and harmonica playing and telling stories about his life?

No brilliant answers came to him before he fell asleep.

VI

Barry drove to the country club earlier than usual on Monday morning. He was about to deliver bad news, and for some reason he didn't want to find Bill waiting in the parking lot for him. He bought a newspaper on the way, turned to the classified ads, and scanned the first two columns while he waited for Bill.

If he were an engineer or an accountant, or an experienced salesman he could probably auction off his services to the highest bidder. But there were no ads for amateur filmmakers.

Management trainee wanted. College degree preferred. Ask for Mr. Seligman.

Barry was circling the ad when Bill suddenly materialized at the side window, grinning happily, holding a piece of paper in his hand. Barry rolled down the window.

"Hey, buddy, hey, buddy," Bill said in his childish voice. "I'm sure glad to see you."

Before Barry could answer, Bill shuffled around and climbed in the passenger side.

"Bill," Barry said, "I want to talk to you seriously today."

Bill paid no attention to him; he was too excited about the piece of paper in his hand. "I made this list here of the things I have to get," he said, "and you can help me get 'em, buddy."

"Bill, listen to me!"

The sharp tone stopped Bill short. His mouth moved and he turned away, not knowing how to respond for a moment. Barry took a deep breath, but Bill thrust his sheet of paper out before Barry could speak.

"You're my buddy," he said meekly, "so I thought maybe you could read this for me."

Barry took the paper. There were scrawls and scratches across it. They looked like Egyptian hieroglyphics. "What is this?" Barry said.

Bill pointed to the spirals and crooked rectangles at the top. "That there...that there is toothpaste. I gotta get toothpaste because my teeth hurt."

Barry looked at the other gibberish. "Bill, this is all nonsense."

"You're right, buddy, you're right." Bill nodded vigorously. "I says to myself this morning, 'Bill, you can't be dumb all your life. Your buddy Barry'll teach you how to read a good book.'" He smiled happily and took his list back, suddenly rocking back and forth.

It was not the best time in the world to give the poor guy a kick in the pants. But there would probably never be a best time. Barry started the car. "All right, I'm gonna drive you into town. But I want you to listen to me, okay?"

"You betcha, buddy. Springtime in the Rockies. We're on the way."

Bill was in no mood to listen. He was going to Disneyland again. With Bill singing "You Are My Sunshine," Barry drove out of the parking lot and headed downtown.

Barry went into the drugstore with him, but he let Bill pick out all the items on the list. "How long have your teeth been hurting?" he asked as Bill pondered over the toothpaste display.

"They always hurt," Bill said. "Ever since I got 'em they hurt. They're real good teeth, and they work real good chewin' things up. But they hurt."

"They hurt bad?"

"Oh . . ." Bill shrugged. "They only hurt when I got 'em in my mouth. They don't hurt when they're in the glass of water."

Barry laughed. He was going to miss old Bill. "Why don't you get some new teeth?"

Apparently such an idea had never occurred to Bill. "Yes, that's what I should do, get some new teeth. I should put that on my list too."

"The County should get them for you, Bill."

Bill nodded, but the idea obviously puzzled him.

"I'll see about getting you some teeth," Barry said.

Bill seemed relieved. "Thank you very much," he said. "You're my real buddy."

He spent an hour gathering up all the items on his list. Then Barry helped him get the correct amount of money from his wallet, and Bill shuffled happily out of the store clutching his bag of treasures.

"Hey, this is good," Bill bubbled. "Thank you for the shaving cream and the gargle and everything. It's good."

"All the important stuff," Barry said.

"That's right. All the important things."

"Buddy," Barry said as they strolled toward the car. "You know I'm a married man, right?"

Bill nodded vigorously. "You should be very happy."

"Right. I am. And you know . . . a married man's gotta take care of his family."

"Right. I know all about that. A married man has gotta take care of his family."

"So I'm going to be looking for a job, Bill. You understand?"

"Sure. You're gonna look for a job."

"Yeah."

"Good." Bill opened his bag and peered in.

"I gotta find a job so I can take care of Sweetie," Barry said. "And the baby when it comes."

"You have lots to do," Bill said. He pulled the bottle of Listerine from the bag, unscrewed the cap, and sniffed at it.

"So that means there are going to be some changes."

Bill was silent, and Barry looked over at him. "Hey, what're you doing?"

Bill had the Listerine bottle tilted to his mouth and was chug-a-lugging it like beer. He pulled the bottle down, half the liquid gone. "This is good stuff, buddy. Thanks for buying it for me."

"You're not supposed to drink that stuff. You just slosh it around and spit it out. It kills germs."

Bill frowned at the bottle. "Yeah?"

"Yeah."

"Oh. Sure." He screwed the cap on and nodded. "Slosh and spit, slosh and spit. Kills germs deader than a door." He returned the bottle to the bag and smiled questioningly at Barry.

It was time to do it, Barry decided. "Listen, buddy. I'm going to have to find a job. And while I'm looking, and after I go to work, there isn't going to be any more filming. So it's gonna be six weeks, a couple of months, maybe longer. So I'm not gonna be able to see you for a while."

It sank in slowly. Bill gave him a puzzled look, then frowned at the pavement for a minute. When he looked back his eyes were distant and full of hurt. "No more *Bill Show*?"

"Not for a while."

Bill started to speak, but his voice choked. He walked on, his head lowered, tightly gripping his bag of goodies. When they reached the car, he turned abruptly, his face flushed. "If we're not doing *The Bill Show* no more," he said hoarsely, "then I'm going to see my sister Sarah."

"Your sister?"

"Yes. She lives over on Florida Street."

Barry was flabbergasted. Bill had not mentioned his sister since their visit to Grandville. Nor had there been any picture or address in his wallet. "Are you sure?"

Bill nodded. "Yes."

"I've never heard of Florida Street. Where is it?"

The question stopped Bill cold for a minute. He stared at Barry, then turned abruptly and opened the car door. "I'll show you," he said. He slid onto the seat, slammed the door and stared silently through the windshield.

Was it possible? Barry circled around to the other side, got in and started the car. "Which way?"

"You just go straight ahead. You just go up to the corner and turn that way. I'll show you."

It seemed impossible. Even if Bill's sister lived in Minneapolis, Barry couldn't believe Bill knew where her house was. Bill didn't know one street from another, and if he went more than a block from the country club he couldn't find his way back. On the other hand, it would certainly solve a lot of problems if he really had a sister nearby.

Barry turned at the first street. It was a residential area with white frame houses and little gardens. "Now where?"

Bill was rocking gently in the seat. "This way," he said. He pointed to the right. "Up this street."

Barry turned again. "Are you sure you know where you're going?"

Bill nodded. "Just some more streets." He looked at the houses on either side, then turned sharply and pointed off toward a side street on the right. "There she is!" he exclaimed. "There she is, Barry!"

Barry hit the brakes and stopped a few feet past the street. Bill immediately pushed the door open and jumped out. "Sarah! Sarah!" he called out.

The side street sloped upward, and an elderly woman pulling a little shopping cart was making her way up the hill. "Sarah!" Bill shouted as he chased after her. "Sarah! It's me, Bill!"

Barry jumped out of the car and chased after him.

The woman turned a half minute before Bill reached her. She was probably in her late fifties, a white-haired, neatly dressed woman who was obviously returning from the market. Her mouth opened and she caught her breath as she saw Bill striding up the hill toward her. "Please!" she cried out and backed away. "I don't have any money! I don't have any money!"

"Sarah!" Bill grabbed the woman's arm as she tried to retreat.

"I'm not Sarah," the terrified woman said. "I'm Aida. Please!"

Barry grabbed Bill's wrist and drew him away. "Bill, I think you've made a mistake. I'm sorry, ma'am. He thought you were somebody else."

The woman continued backing away. She looked from Bill to Barry, still uncertain about them, then turned and hurried up the hill with her cart.

Bill stared numbly after her, breathing hard, too confused to speak.

"You've just made a mistake, Bill. Come on. It's all right. Just a mistake."

"I know," Bill said hoarsely.

"Come on, buddy. I'll take you home."

Bill turned and went limply down the hill with him. "I thought it was Sarah," he said. "I thought it was Sarah." He seemed amazed by his own mistake, as if there had been absolutely no doubt in his mind two minutes ago.

"It's okay, Bill. Let's go home, shall we?"

Bill was silent all the way back to the country club. He placed his bag from the drugstore on his lap and gazed vacantly out the window, making only vague responses to Barry's conversation. He looked like a man who had just learned the world was coming to an end, and he didn't have anybody to say goodbye to.

"It's not going to be so bad, Bill," Barry said. "I'll

come and see you as often as I can. And some day we'll finish *The Bill Show*."

When he left him at the country club, Bill said nothing and trudged off toward the kitchen without turning back.

Interviewing for a job was as miserable as Barry remembered it. He had called Mr. Seligman and went over and filled out an application form. "You've been a free-lance cameraman?" Mr. Seligman asked suspiciously. "And I suppose if business picks up at the television station, you'll want to go back to that."

"Not necessarily," Barry said.

Mr. Seligman owned a garment manufacturing company that produced stocking caps, and had about six employees. He looked like a bookkeeper in a Charles Dickens novel.

"Well, I'm afraid 'not necessarily' is insufficient in this instance, Mr. Morrow. If I invest in a young man I expect some return on that investment."

The heavy investment Mr. Seligman had in mind was minimum wage for the first three months. Barry decided not to devote his life to stocking caps.

Salesman wanted, no experience necessary. Fabulous earnings.

A man named "Harv" told Barry to come right over to the Wickham Hotel, suite four-fourteen for an interview.

Harv was a go-getter in his mid-twenties, wearing a plaid jacket, a turtleneck sweater and penny loafers. Along with a sales crew of five or six men, Harv went out in the farm country every week and sold farmers' wives on the idea of having those old snapshots of grandma and grandpa enlarged to beautiful eleven-by-fourteen prints, and then tinted by expert artists. It was a great racket, and the hicks out in the country gobbled it up. Harv's boys worked on straight commission, and some of them made as much as a thousand dollars a week. They stayed in motels during the week and they had a great time together.

Barry told Harv he would think about it.

"Let me know by six o'clock tonight," Harv said. "We're all heading out for Sauk Rapids, over in Benton County first thing in the morning."

Barry promised to let him know, and walked two blocks down the street to a place called the Lambert Employment Agency.

"Do you know how to operate computers?" the interviewer asked after she looked over his application.

"Sure," Barry said. It was stretching the truth a little, but maybe it would lead to something. His experience with computers had been limited to entering names into a computer in the admissions office at the University of Minnesota.

"Good," the girl said. "I think I have something for you right now. Do you have a car?"

The Twin Cities Data Processing Service was on the west side of town on the third floor of a steel and glass bank building. Barry filled out an application, noting his six months of computer experience at the TV station, and was then introduced to Mr. Dobson in the insurance division, where they did data processing for insurance companies. Mr. Dobson looked like Mr. Seligman's twin brother. "So, you've had six months of computer work, Mr. Morrow?"

"More or less."

"I see. And what kind of computers did you operate?"

Mr. Dobson was standing in front of a big computer panel that said IBM over the keyboard. "Burroughs," he answered.

"I see. Hmmm. Well, I suppose we're going to have to train you all over again."

"I suppose so," Barry said. "But I'm sure I'll pick it up fast."

From there Barry went directly to the local IBM

service offices and picked up a handful of booklets on computer operation. Then he bought a small bottle of champagne and headed for home.

VII

The County Welfare Department was crowded. At least a hundred people were waiting in lines, or sitting at tables filling out forms, baring their souls to the mercy of the Hennepin County bureaucracy. It was noon, the floor was littered with trash, and an air of hopelessness filled the huge waiting room.

Barry waited patiently in line to reach the information desk, and then asked to see Miss Keating.

Miss Keating was on the fifth floor, the young lady informed him. He would have to go up there and arrange an appointment.

The fifth floor was quieter, and the receptionist buzzed Miss Keating and relayed Barry's request for an interview. Two minutes later Miss Keating appeared, rolling a ballpoint pen impatiently through her fingers. "You want to talk to me about Bill Sackter?" she asked.

She was a slender black woman—in her mid-forties, Barry guessed. She was dressed neatly in a brown skirt and matching jacket, but she had a defensive air about her, as if she wanted no outside interference with her work.

"That's right," Barry said. "My name is Barry Morrow, and I'm a friend of Bill's. I understand you're his case worker."

"Is there some problem with Bill?" she asked.

"Sort of. Could we go somewhere and talk, Miss Keating?"

She frowned and looked him over. He was dressed for work, wearing a clean shirt and pants. Apparently he passed the inspection. "Very well," she said.

Her office was one of a dozen simply furnished cubicles along a narrow corridor. She sat down behind a desk piled high with manila folders, and Barry took one of the two wooden chairs.

"Now what's the problem, Mr. Morrow?"

Miss Keating was obviously a person who didn't waste the taxpayers' money with small talk. That was fine with Barry. "Bill needs new dentures," he said.

Her eyes flickered for an instant. "Are you a dentist, Mr. Morrow?"

"No. But I don't have to be a dentist to know his teeth are a mess. What I need is some kind of form stating that Bill is a ward of the State, and therefore entitled to new dentures."

Miss Keating stared at him for a minute, then swung around and dug a manila folder out of a file cabinet. She opened it and consulted some papers. "I don't see your name on the list of Bill's family and friends," she said.

"We're new friends."

"And Bill has been a ward of the State for many years."

"What does that have to do with it? His teeth are a mess and he needs new ones."

She slowly closed the folder and sat back, her fingers laced together. It was interrogation time. "Where are you coming from, Mr. Morrow?" she asked. "Are you in the habit of walking into the welfare office during your lunch hour to take up the cause of a stray, retarded old man?"

"I told you; we're friends."

"I see," she said dubiously. "And what's in this for you?"

"Nothing."

"Nothing?"

"Yeah. I'm a filmmaker, and—"

"Oh, I see," she said with a cold smile. "You're the one who's doing a film about Bill. He mentioned something about that."

"Yes, and I think there's great potential in the project."

"A great potential for you. But what about Bill?"

"I think there's a great potential for Bill, too," Barry said. "I think it's a good experience for him, relating to people and the world around him. I think the benefits for Bill are already apparent."

She nodded, unconvinced. "Films end, Mr. Morrow, and so do friendships. Now where is this supposed to leave Bill when it's all over?"

"With a new set of teeth, for one thing," Barry said. "And perhaps a new sense of his own worth."

"And perhaps you will make a great deal of money. Is that what you have in mind?"

"If I make a great deal of money, Bill will certainly share it, Miss Keating," he said, trying to control his temper. "Contrary to what you're suggesting, I don't want to exploit him. I'm his friend and intend to continue being his friend as long as he wants it that way. And being his friend, I don't like him to be in pain all the time. All I want is for the State to give him a new set of dentures. It's very simple, Miss Keating. And you being his welfare caseworker, I presume you are interested in his welfare. Therefore, it would seem to me that you would want him to have new dentures also."

To her credit, she didn't get angry. She pondered the situation a moment, then turned and dropped the folder back in the file drawer.

"I've had a lot of trouble with Bill over the last couple of years," she said quietly. "Arrests, joblessness. And he has an ulcer condition on his leg. I have to tell you that Bill needs the same kind of constant care a child needs."

Barry glanced at his watch and nodded. He was going to be late getting back from his lunch hour. "All I want is new teeth for Bill, Miss Keating."

She pulled open a drawer of her desk and brought out a form. "All right, Mr. Morrow, I'll authorize the necessary dental work. But I want you to know that any additional filming can only be done with written authorization from this department."

"There will be no more filming," Barry said.

She busied herself filling out the form. "In the future, the Department of Social Services—"

"—has no business telling me who my friends can be," Barry said.

She looked up sharply from the papers. "Your friends?"

"Yes. My friend, Bill."

"Tell me, Mr. Morrow," she said with a long sigh, "would you invite Bill home to meet your parents?"

Barry started to answer, then closed his mouth. He hadn't pictured somebody like Bill sitting in his parents' dining room. "I think so," he said weakly.

She nodded and returned to her papers. "Think about it, Mr. Morrow. In the meantime, I'll get an okay on this form and see that Bill gets to a dentist."

Barry thought about it on the way back to his office, and through the rest of the afternoon. He had arrived late, and Mr. Dobson looked pointedly at his watch and scowled a warning to let Barry know his transgression was major and duly noted. But after that Mr. Dobson left him alone.

Barry was being taught how to operate the computers by a young genius named Nick Ellis, who was sympathetic enough to cover for Barry's ignorance, and after six weeks of it, Barry was holding his own.

When he arrived home that night, Bev was lying on her back, alternately lifting her knees up to her burgeoning belly.

"Hi, how was work?" she grunted between puffs.

"Not too bad. I've been programmed to say, 'Work is wonderful.'" He dropped his voice into a flat computer sound. "'I am an important cog in the wheels of industry. My work is good. I like my work. I will never ask for a raise, and I will never say anything unkind about Mr. Dobson. He is a fine man with a heart of gold, and I should never be late and make him unhappy.'"

Bev laughed and lifted another knee. "Come on, you're supposed to be doing this with me."

Barry poured himself a glass of super pulverized tomato-carrot juice and drank it. "Why?"

"Shared experience. Remember?"

According to the book on healthy, painless childbirth, prospective fathers were supposed to do all the exercises and eat the same things as the mothers. Which meant, Barry supposed, that he would also have labor pains when the time came. But it probably wouldn't hurt after sitting in front of a computer console all day. He stretched out beside her.

"Okay," she said, "you've got to push your back into the floor. Like this."

Barry did it, then rolled over and kissed her. "I know another good exercise," he suggested.

She laughed and pushed him away. "And then you've got to breathe like this. Use the floor for resistance, not me."

"That's no fun."

"It's not meant to be fun."

Barry rolled away, put his hands behind his head and squinted at the ceiling. "I've been thinking."

"About what?" she said between puffs.

"About having lunch with my parents on Sunday."

"That's pretty heavy thinking—considering we have lunch with them often on Sundays."

"I've been thinking about inviting somebody to go with us."

"Who?"

"A friend."

"That sounds mysterious. Does the friend have a name?"

"Yeah. Bill Sackter."

She stopped exercising and stared at him. "Bill Sackter?"

Barry smiled. "You with me?"

"You bet I am."

*   *   *

During the next three days Barry vacillated between thinking it was a brilliant idea, and that it was the
stupidest thing he had ever done in his life. His parents
were not snobs, or bigots, or cold-hearted ogres. But
neither were they liberal-minded do-gooders who spent
their free time ladling out soup at the midnight mis-
sion. His father was the owner of a medium-sized
distribution company that sold housewares and appli-
ances to retail dealers in seven midwestern states. Quietly
proud of his success, he had worked hard for what he
had, and he saw no reason why everyone else shouldn't
work as hard if they expected to be successful. There
was nothing wrong with such a philosophy. But in his
concern over practicing the good old American virtues,
not much thought was ever given to people like Bill
who were left at the starting line because they didn't
have the mental or physical equipment to participate in
the race. And hard work and success, as it did with
people in any enterprise, brought him into daily contact with only those people who shared his philosophy.
His father gave to charity, vaguely knowing that somewhere out in the world there were people who needed
that charity. But the closest he might ever come to a
person like Bill would be if he accidentally wandered
into the kitchen of a country club, or if one of them
came to the back door asking for a handout.

Barry's mother, on the other hand, had a bit of a
pollyannaish view toward life. All people were good
until they proved otherwise, and Bill would certainly be
welcome in their house until he started smashing the good
china or pinching the ladies' bottoms. But her contact with
people who were "different" was probably limited to one
of her suburban neighbors who might have a trace of
Italian or Greek blood in her distant ancestry.

Bill was all dressed up in a jacket and a necktie
when Bev and Barry picked him up at the country club.
He came shuffling out to the car, his wig squarely on

top of his head, and three or four bits of toilet paper stuck to his face where he'd cut himself shaving.

"You look very nice, Bill," Bev said as he jumped into the back seat.

"Thank you very much," he said automatically. "Ol' Bill goin' to dinner in a regular house with good people."

"Don't get too excited," Bev said as they drove out of the parking lot. "They're just family."

"Okay, Sweetie," he said. "Can I play my harmonica?"

"Sure. Wouldn't be a party without music."

Barry thought it might be less of a shock to his mother and father if Bill arrived without his fright-wig. And it might be a good idea to remove the bits of toilet paper. But the suggestions could wait until they reached the house.

"Wouldn't be a party without music," Bill agreed. "Hey, buddy. I'm as happy as a lard."

"You can't get much happier than a . . . lard," Barry said.

"Hey, buddy," Bill said, suddenly sounding worried. "Can your ma cook?"

Bev and Barry laughed. "She's a good cook, Bill," Bev assured him.

"That's good. That's real good. Good food in a regular house with good people. Can't get any better than that."

Bill sat back, satisfied, and pulled out his harmonica. "William, Bill for short," he said as if practicing for when he was introduced to Barry's parents. Then he puffed a few notes on the harmonica and launched into a spirited version of "She'll Be Coming Around the Mountain When She Comes."

Bev and Barry sang along with him as they skimmed down the freeway. "Hey, these are nice houses!" Bill said when they reached the suburbs. "I'd like to live in a house like these. They all got grass and flowers. I saw a man once with a flower in his jacket. It was red." He started "Coming Around the Mountain" again as Barry pulled into the driveway. Then he quickly stuck the harmonica in his pocket. "Hey, this is nice."

Barry turned in the seat and saw that Bill was breathing hard, growing excited over their arrival. "Easy, Bill," he said soothingly. "How about if we take those bits of paper off your face? I think the cuts are all dried now."

Bill thrust his chin out and let him remove the bits.

"Now," Barry said, "I want to talk to you before we go in, okay?"

"Sure, buddy, sure."

Barry glanced at Bev and put a hand on Bill's shoulder. "Bill, I think it would be best if... if you left your wig in the car."

Bill's face reddened and he shrank back, staring at the floor. "The false wig?" he mumbled as if he'd been asked to remove his pants.

"Yeah, the false wig."

"Well, I don't know," Bill said, agitated. "People don't like me as much when I don't have my false wig on."

"Sure they do. You look better, and they like you better."

Bill glanced at the house and fidgeted. He smoothed his pants and shifted in the seat. "Well...no...you see the false wig goes on top of the head...see, like this, see...and a good man's got to have good hair."

"What makes you think that?" Barry asked.

"A good man's got good hair. You've got hair."

"Yeah, but I'm young."

Bill frowned. "I'm young," he protested. "I'm a spring chicken."

Barry stared at him and Bill sagged like a balloon with a fast leak. Somehow he'd convinced himself that he was nothing without his wig.

"All right," Bev said and gave him a smile. "Let's go. The wig looks fine, Bill."

"Bev!" Barry protested.

Bill was suddenly all smiles again. Both he and Bev

pushed their doors open and got out. "All right," Bill said happily. "How sweet it is! Let's rip-snort and toot!"

He'd lost the battle, Barry realized. He grabbed the bouquet of flowers from the back seat, slid out the door and caught up with Bev. "What'd you do that for? He looks ridiculous."

"Now's not the time," she said. "Bill's not worried about it. Why are you so uptight and nervous?"

It was true, Barry realized. He was more tense than Bill.

Barry's mother answered the door, all smiles and hospitality. She was an attractive woman in her early fifties, with neatly coiffed gray hair and wearing her Sunday best.

Almost imperceptibly, her smile stiffened for an instant, but she quickly recovered. "You must be Barry's friend, Bill," she said sweetly and extended her hand. "I'm Rosenell Morrow, his mother."

Bill gave her hand a shake, smiling happily under his wig. "Say, glad to meet you, Mrs. Moore. Bill for short. Say, this is a beautiful house. You really must be rich!" He turned nervously and pointed at Barry. "Barry brought some flowers. Said it was a surprise!"

"Oh, how beautiful. Thank you, dear. Hello, Bev, darling. You look radiant, just the way an expectant mother is supposed to look." she gave Barry and Bev kisses and they moved inside where Barry's father was waiting in his country club blazer. "Robert, this is Barry's friend, Bill," Mrs. Morrow said.

"Bill for short," Bill said and stuck out a hand.

Barry's father shook the hand and nodded, smiling uncertainly. "Nice to meet you, Bill."

"Say, this is a beautiful house," Bill said again. "You really must be rich."

"Thank you," Mr. Morrow murmured.

"Thank you very much," Bill said almost as a reflex action.

"Now, why don't you all go out on the terrace while

I put these flowers in some water," Mrs. Morrow said. "Then I'll bring us some lemonade."

"Well, now," Barry's father said when they were all seated on the terrace, "I understand you and Barry have been making a film together, Bill."

Bill was still nervous, glancing around at the potted plants as if they were about to jump on him. "Uh-huh. *The Bill Show.* Like *I Dream of Jeanie.* But we're not making it anymore. And I'm getting some new teeth. The ones I have hurt."

Barry smiled, partly at Bill's non sequiturs and partly at his father's hopeless attempt to make normal conversation with Bill.

"How's business, dad?" he asked to take the pressure off.

"Good, very good as a matter of fact. Considering the way the economy is floundering, we're doing very well."

Bill stared at him. "Are you a company?" he asked.

Mr. Morrow blinked and threw an uneasy glance at Barry. "I'm the president of one," he said.

"No kidding," Bill said, continuing to stare. He had never seen a president before.

Mrs. Morrow arrived with a tray of lemonade and passed it around. "This is good, Mrs. Moore," Bill said before he tasted it. "I like lemonade. Thank you very much."

"Thank you, Bill," she said sweetly.

"Well, Barry," Mr. Morrow said and turned away from Bill, "have you heard anything about that media position yet?"

Barry had forgotten about the application he'd sent to University of Iowa. Carl Amundsen had told him about the position after seeing an ad in one of the television trade journals. The University was looking for someone with industry experience to teach a class in media communications with an emphasis on film and television production. Barry had little confidence in his prospects, but wanted to sound positive and enthusiastic when he discussed it with his father. "I haven't heard anything yet," he said.

His father nodded. "If you're interested in continuing in computer work, I have some friends who may be of some use to you."

Continuing to work with computers would make his father happier than anything—a growing industry with lots of security and opportunity for advancement. "No, dad," he said. "I want to stay with film."

His disappointment was obvious. "We thought you might have changed your mind about that," he said.

Bill was fidgeting, as if anxious to participate in the conversation. He quickly jumped in when he saw an opportunity. "No, he don't want to change his mind," he said gravely. "We're going to do *The Bill Show*. It's going to be a real good show with lots of singing and playing the harmonica. We went to Grandville too. That's how Barry and me met. We're buddies now, and I'm gonna get some new teeth." Bill nodded and looked around nervously, then pulled out his harmonica.

"Not now, Bill," Barry said quietly.

Bill looked hurt, as if he'd been chastised. He nodded and returned the harmonica to his pocket. "Not now," he said.

"Well, I think lunch is all ready if everybody's hungry," Mrs. Morrow said cheerfully.

Bill rose and marched into the dining room and sat down. Barry smiled as his father gave him a questioning look, and they all moved toward the dining room. "He'll be all right, dad. He just likes to eat."

"Does he live in some kind of institution?"

"No, he lives at the Minikahda Country Club. He works in their kitchen."

"I see," Mr. Morrow said, as if that gave him something to think about.

Bill sat quietly watching Bev and Mrs. Morrow bring the food in from the kitchen. When they were all seated, Mrs. Morrow handed him a steaming dish of beans.

"Ummm, green beans," he said. "They're good for you. I like green beans."

"Have lots of them, Bill," she said. "We've got plenty more."

Bill heaped the side of his plate with beans. "I like green beans. Thank you very much."

"Well, how about it?" Mrs. Morrow said to Bev. "Are you going to have a natural childbirth, or that new French method everyone's talking about where they dump the baby in water the moment it's born?"

"Oh, you mean the Leboyer method. Well, Barry and I have discussed it, and—"

"Ummm, sweet potatoes," Bill said as Mrs. Morrow ladled the potatoes from the platter for him. "I'll have thirty."

"He means one," Barry said.

"He means two or three," Bev corrected.

"Then I'll give him four," Mrs. Morrow said.

"Have you known each other long?" Mr. Morrow asked.

"Oh, about five months," Barry answered. "Isn't that right, Bill?"

"We've been buddies a long time," Bill said as Mrs. Morrow passed him the platter of chicken. "Oh, look at that chicken! Isn't that good!"

"Help yourself, Bill. There's plenty."

Bill transferred two pieces to his plate, then reached for a third.

"Go easy on that," Barry cautioned.

Bill held his fork uncertainly over the platter. He knew Barry was saying no, but he couldn't resist the temptation. "It's good chicken," he said and took another piece.

"Bill!" Barry gave him a hard look, then smiled at his mother. "Bill's on a diet. He's watching his weight. Isn't that right, Bill?"

Bill shook his head. "I'm not watching my weight now. I'm gonna nab more chicken." He spared another piece and dropped it on his already-heaping plate.

"Put that back!" Barry commanded.

The harsh tone seemed to confuse Bill. As if to calm his sudden agitation, he quickly transferred another piece of chicken to his plate. "I'm gonna have more chicken."

Bev suppressed a smile as Barry's father and mother stared with astonishment.

"Bill, put that back!" Barry said firmly.

Bill turned and stared at him as if suddenly realizing he had done something wrong. He opened his mouth and closed it, then looked at his plate and at the platter. He hunched down lower, his eyes almost closed as his jaw worked defiantly backward and forward. As if compelled to take some action, he reached over for the platter, brought it to his plate and tilted all of the remaining chicken onto the stack in front of him. It tumbled down over the already overburdened plate and slid onto the tablecloth and into his lap. His face contorted, then he rose abruptly and marched off into the kitchen.

They all gazed incredulously at the mess he'd left behind. "Your friend seems to be very upset," Mrs. Morrow murmured uncertainly.

"Maybe an occasion like this is a little too much for him to handle," her husband suggested.

Barry sat numbly, torn between anger and embarrassment. Bill had never done a thing like this before. It was almost as if he'd deliberately tried to humiliate him.

"Go talk to him, Barry," Bev said.

"No," Barry said defiantly. Why should he? Bill knew better than to do such a stupid thing.

"He just got too excited," Bev said to the others. "He's like a little child."

"Of course," Mrs. Morrow said. She left her chair and knelt by the table, cleaning the carpet with her napkin. "It's all right. No harm done."

Barry watched her for a minute, then pushed his chair back. "Excuse me," he said.

Bill was standing just inside the kitchen door, his head lowered so far his wig was almost falling off.

"Bill?" Barry said softly, "I'm sorry. I didn't mean to yell at you like that."

Bill kept his head down. "It's my fault, too," he mumbled hoarsely. "I shouldn't have run away from a good buddy who's trying to help me. I'm sorry."

"Come on. Let's go eat."

Bill didn't move. He looked like he was trying to shrink away to nothing.

"It's okay, Bill. Nobody's upset, and Mom is glad you like the chicken so much. She wants you to eat it."

Bill glanced up cautiously, as if trying to determine if Barry was telling the truth.

"It's all right, Bill. They like you very much. And they like your wig."

Bill lifted his head and touched his wig, then rocked his head from side to side, smiling a little. "Okay," he said happily. "Let's go eat."

He was a model guest for the rest of the afternoon. He apologized over and over again to Mrs. Morrow, and he wouldn't eat any more food unless somebody else put it on his plate. After lunch he played his harmonica and sang, and by the time they left, he'd almost completely won over his hosts.

VIII

The baby came six weeks later. Until he received the call, it had been a bad day for Barry. A week earlier he had given the company's telephone number to Bill, and every time the old guy was feeling low and wanted company, he got somebody at the country club to dial the phone for him.

He made three calls that day, and by the time Barry answered the third one, Mr. Dobson was glaring bullets from across the computer room. For some reason, no matter how hard he worked, Barry never could get a smile out of Arthur Dobson. He had a hunch Dobson was saving up for one king-sized smile on the day he handed Barry his pink slip.

"You haven't come to see me, buddy," Bill moaned over the phone. "I'm just a crackminded old man and nobody wants to talk to me anymore."

"No," Barry said in a hushed tone, trying to pretend it was a business call. "You're not a crackminded old man, Bill. It's just that Bev is gonna have a baby any day now, and I've got to make some money. More cush."

"Let's go for a ride, buddy. I want to go for a ride because the sun is shining. Like it was Sunday."

"Bill, I can't take you for a ride. And I gotta get back to work."

"I'm a regular good man," Bill said.

"Right. You're a regular good man. Goodbye, Bill. I gotta go now."

"I gotta get some Polident."

"Okay, I'll get you some Polident, Bill. Now I—"

"I'm just an old bean and you don't want to see me."

Barry had to cut it off; Mr. Dobson had risen from his desk and was strolling across the room toward him. "No, you're not an old bean, Bill, and I'll see you as soon as I can. You're a regular good guy, and I'll bring you some Polident tonight. Goodbye, Bill."

He hung up and swung back to his computer console, but Dobson was still coming.

"Well, well, Mr. Morrow, aren't we busy enough? Let's see, you've been here six weeks now, haven't you? Maybe it's time for your own personal phone."

Barry gave him a big smile. "I just love this job, Mr. Dobson."

Dobson nodded. "I can see why. No other employer would give you so much free time to make your social calls."

"It was sort of . . . sort of an emergency."

74

"I see. With all the emergencies you handle, perhaps you should join the fire department's rescue squad."

"I'm sorry."

Mr. Dobson sucked in a chestful of air and headed back to his desk, where the telephone was buzzing. Barry turned to his computer console again.

"Oh, Mr. Morrow," Dobson said sourly from across the room, "I'm sorry to bother you, but you have another call. Line three."

Barry gritted his teeth, punched the lighted button and picked up the phone. If it was Bill he was going to slam it down again.

"Barry?"

It was his mother. "Yeah?"

"Bev just called. She's going into labor, and she's going to the hospital."

"She is? Where? Who's taking her?"

"One of your neighbors, I guess. Mrs. O'Brien?"

"Yeah. Okay, I'm on my way."

Barry slammed down the phone, grabbed his jacket and grinned from ear-to-ear. "The baby! A baby!! I'm gonna be a father!"

A chorus of cheers came from the other operators— all except Dobson, who sighed wearily as Barry passed.

It was a seven pound, two ounce baby boy with an incredibly loud voice. He announced his presence in the world at seven-fifteen that night, and Bev came through the ordeal with flying colors.

The next day Barry handed out cigars, including one to Mr. Dobson, who told everyone not to smoke those "damned things" in the office. That night Barry delivered the Polident to Bill and told him the good news, then picked him up on Saturday after they'd brought the baby home.

"I want you to be the first to see him, because you're an uncle now, Bill."

"Yeah, an uncle," Bill said. "Uncle Bill for short."

"He's almost as good-looking as you are."

"Does he have any hair?" Bill asked after a thoughtful silence.

"Not very much. About the same as you. He's a regular good guy."

That seemed to please Bill.

At first the baby frightened him. It was as if he'd never seen such a thing before. He stood halfway across the room and peered at it, then slowly edged closer. "What's his name?" he asked.

"Clayton. Clay for short."

"Clay for short," he said. "I can say that."

He peered more closely at it, but kept his hands behind him, as if it were something incredibly delicate and precious that he might break if he touched it. "He's beautiful," he finally said with a look of awe. Then he frowned and looked gravely at Bev. "He doesn't have any teeth."

"No, it'll be a while before he has any teeth," Bev said.

"Just like me."

"That's right. Just like his Uncle Bill."

A week later Bill was holding him and occasionally feeding him. But when the baby cried, he got a look of panic and quickly handed him over to Bev or Barry, as if he'd been responsible for the outburst. Then he played his harmonica or sang until the baby was quiet again.

The world was full of surprises, and sometimes when the stars were all in the right place the pleasant ones came at exactly the right time.

There was no way Barry could stop Bill from calling his office. Bill would solemnly agree never to do it again, and then would forget about it an hour later and be back on the phone again. Three weeks after the baby was born, Mr. Dobson quit glaring, but Barry knew his days were numbered. Suddenly Dobson was wearing a smug smile, and Barry knew that somebody upstairs had probably agreed with Dobson, and the pink slip was in the payroll department all ready to be clipped to his next paycheck.

And then it came! A fat envelope with the words *University of Iowa* printed on the upper left corner. It could have been a catalog offering courses Barry might be interested in. Or maybe a packet of brochures extolling the University's virtues, and suggesting that young Clayton Morrow enroll for the class of 2002.

Instead, it was a fat contract, along with a short letter from a man named Thomas Walz, Director of the School of Social Work. "Dear Mr. Morrow: I am pleased to inform you that..."

"Oh, my God!" Barry exclaimed and sat bolt upright.

Bev came out of the bathroom with Clay wrapped in towels. "What's the matter? What is it, Barry?"

"University of Iowa," he said, scanning the letter.

"What'd they say? Did they like your presentation?"

"They loved it! They loved the film, they loved the slides! They loved everything!"

"Oh, my God!" Still holding Clay, Bev dropped on the couch beside him and peered at the letter.

"Eighteen thousand a year!" Barry said. "Eighteen thousand dollars! I'm a real person. We can get credit, buy a new car... go back into debt."

Bev laughed and gave him a kiss. "Where's University of Iowa?"

"I don't know. Probably in Iowa somewhere."

They celebrated through the afternoon, mostly buying new clothes for Clay. On Monday morning, Barry beat Mr. Dobson to the punch and ruined his day by resigning his position. Then, more soberly, he drove to the country club, knowing Bill was going to be crushed by the news that he and Bev and Clay were going to leave Minneapolis.

By setting aside *The Bill Show* project and getting a job, Barry had already partially severed the cord with Bill. Since Clay had arrived, the number of phone calls to the office had dropped to two or three a week, and

Bill seemed reconciled to less attention. On the other hand, he spent more time with them on weekends, and Clay had also become Bill's "Uncle Buddy." Barry didn't look forward to breaking the bad news to him.

As usual, Bill was in the kitchen methodically scrubbing a stack of pots and pans. Barry was reminded of the first time he came into this kitchen and saw Bill standing at the sink, and the other man yelling at him and ridiculing him for not knowing how to read the clock. Barry took a deep breath and crossed the room to his side.

"Oh, hi, buddy," Bill said. He lifted a soapy hand to his head and adjusted his wig. "We gonna go see Clay?"

"No, not today, Bill. I want to talk to you for a minute. It's about something ... something important."

"Oh, okay." Bill set the pot aside and dried his hands. "You gonna wash all those pans all by yourself?"

"Yeah," he said and nodded. "I'll clean 'em up good. That's my job."

Barry wasn't sure how to phrase it; no matter what he said, it wasn't going to be pleasant for Bill. "Listen ... you know I've been looking for work ... trying to get a better job than I have at the computer company. I've been sending out applications and presentations to various places, and so forth."

"You told me that, buddy. That's good."

"Right. Well, I got a better job. A job that I think I'm going to like."

"That's good. I like my job too."

Bill wasn't making it any easier. "Yeah. Well, the point is, this job isn't in Minneapolis, Bill. It's in Iowa."

Barry waited for a reaction, but none came. "I see," Bill said and nodded.

"What it means, Bill, is that Bev and Clay and I will have to move to Iowa. We can't live in Minneapolis anymore."

It took a minute to sink in. Bill gazed at him and blinked, then looked at the towel in his hands. He frowned, his voice suddenly no more than a whisper. "How far away is this I-O-way?"

"It's not far."

He gave Barry a suspicious glance. "How far?"

"By car, about eight hours."

Bill worked his mouth and picked at his fingers, then moved away along the sink. He stopped at the end, his head down.

"What's the matter, Bill?"

"I feel sick," he said thickly. "I think I got fevers."

Barry felt a little sick himself. "You want to see a doctor?"

"No, no! I don't want to see none of them guys. I just don't feel good." There were tears in his throat now. He turned his back to Barry.

"Bill, Iowa's the next state, just south of here. It's no big deal. We can still visit. We can talk on the phone."

Bill shook his head and sniffled. "No. I can't dial them things. Leave ol' Bill. Leave ol' Bill."

"I'm not leaving because of you."

"Crackminded ol' bean."

"You're not a crackminded ol' bean. But I've got to take care of my family, Bill. I gotta get me a good job, make lots of cash."

Bill dropped the towel on the sink and shook his head. "Low-grade man," he said and stared hopelessly at the floor. "I have a sister in Florida named Sarah." It sounded like he was trying to convince himself he still had some tenuous connection with the human race.

Barry moved closer to him. "Bill, how can I make you understand? We're gonna stay in touch. I'm gonna call you all the time. It's just that I gotta take this job."

He turned away and faced the wall, trembling, trying to hold back the tears.

"Bill...open up, Bill. Come on, I want to talk to you. Bill, please don't take it this way. Come on. I'm not leaving because of you. We're still friends. We're still buddies. But I just gotta take this job."

His head still down, Bill shoved his hands in his

pockets and strode out the door. Barry followed him. "Come on, Bill, don't act like this."

"You don't need to follow me back to my room," Bill said angrily through his tears. "I ain't no dummy. I know my way."

"Of course you're not a dummy. And we're going to stay in touch, Bill. I'll be calling you all the time. But I have to take this job."

Bill kept walking. When he reached the room, he went in quickly and closed the door hard behind him. Barry reached for the knob, then dropped his hand. Somehow it seemed even more heartless to violate Bill's privacy right now. "Bill," he said through the door, "please don't take it this way."

The television suddenly blasted on—some situation comedy with a raucous laugh track punctuating every two seconds of dialogue.

Barry stood outside the door, uncertain what to do. In his present mood, it didn't seem likely that Bill was going to be influenced by anything more Barry had to say. "I'll call you, Bill," Barry shouted through the door.

He waited, but there was no response. Feeling like he had just betrayed his best friend, he finally walked back through the kitchen and out to the parking lot.

IX

When they arrived in Iowa City, they found a livable apartment six blocks from the campus of the University. It was a pretty little town of about fifty thousand people, on the Iowa River. Most of the residents appeared to be students, or connected with the University in one way or another.

School started the day after they arrived, and the first two weeks were hectic. Everybody, including Barry, seemed to be confused or lost; the bookstore didn't seem to have the right textbooks; classes had been changed to different rooms at the last minute, some classes were overcrowded, and at others no students showed up at all. "I'm not sure I'm supposed to be in your class, Mr. Morrow. Can you help me?" "Is this class *Documentary Production One-A,* or *One-B?* I've already taken *One-A.*" "Are you going to grade on a curve, Mr. Morrow? If you are, I'm going to take something else." "Could I take this course in the afternoon instead of morning? The morning conflicts with my English Lit class." "I'm a history major. Do I get upper division credit for your class, Mr. Morrow?"

Tom Walz, the head of the department, assured Barry that it was always this way, and things would settle down by the third week. He told this to Barry with a serene smile while he was hurrying across the campus to fill in for one of his professors who'd gone home with a migraine headache that morning.

In a way, Barry was fortunate. Unlike some of the less popular "required" courses, his students all seemed to be eager to learn about filmmaking, and they all showed up bright and attentive, and hungry for knowledge. Nevertheless, there were those moments of terror when he found fifteen or twenty faces staring at him for the first time, their owners all wondering if he really knew anything about his subject, or if he had any talents at all as a teacher. But the fears and trepidations quickly dissolved, and by the third week things began to swing along at a more relaxed pace.

He had put off calling Bill, partly because he was so busy he didn't have much time to think about what he might say, and partly because of the possibility that a phone call might upset Bill more than it would please him. And in the back of his mind was the thought that on the first free weekend he would drive to Minneapolis and spend a couple of days with him. But for some reason that weekend never seemed to materialize.

* * *

In Minneapolis, Bill Sackter had no thoughts about future weekends. He lived from day to day and from hour to hour, feeling a great aching emptiness in his chest. He worked hard at scrubbing the pots and pans, and got them cleaner than ever before. Harry, the man he worked for, laughed at him because Bill often scrubbed the same pots over and over before they were even used again. But Bill didn't care. If there weren't any dirty pots he scrubbed the clean ones, because that was his job. Sometimes in the mornings he went out to the parking lot and watched for Barry's station wagon to turn into the driveway. But it never came, and after the first two weeks he didn't do it anymore.

In the afternoons he went to his room and watched reruns of *I Dream of Jeanie* and *The Mary Tyler Moore Show* and *Gilligan's Island*. They didn't amuse him as much anymore, but he had nothing else to do. Then he went back to scrubbing pots and pans, paying little attention to Harry's sneers and insults.

One afternoon, while he was drying plates and stacking them on the shelf, Miss Keating suddenly appeared. She came through the dining room door and walked across the room smiling at him.

It was the first time anybody had smiled at him since almost longer than he could remember. Bill felt warm inside. He wiped his hands on his towel and stuck one out. "Hello, Miz Keating."

"Hi, Bill. How are you feeling?"

He patted the top of his head to be sure his wig was straight, and nodded. "I'm just fine, Miz Keating."

She smiled again and leaned against the sink with her arms folded over her chest. "I don't understand, Bill, I heard they gave you a week off, but you didn't take it. You're still working."

He didn't want a week off. He wouldn't have anything to do but sit in his room, and he liked being in the kitchen better. He shrugged. "Work is good for the ticker."

She nodded and looked closely at him. "Listen,

next Monday I've made an appointment at the doctor's for you."

Bill turned away and picked up his towel. "Oh, I don't need to go to no doctor. I'm okay, Miz Keating."

"It's time for your annual checkup. And I want him to look at that leg."

"Ol' Bill's leg is doin' good," he said. "It's a good leg now." It was not true; the leg was hurting him a lot more than it used to. But he didn't want a doctor pushing and scraping at it again. The doctor at Grandville used to put burning stuff all over the sores that made them feel worse than ever.

Miss Keating kept smiling at him—a smile that always meant she was going to have her way no matter what he said. "I know, Bill. But I'd still like the doctor to look at it anyway. Okay?"

Bill turned and wiped the sink with his towel. Barry had left, and now Miss Keating was after him again. Everything was even worse than it was before. "No," he said, "you just want to take me back to that place again."

"What place?"

"I don't want to say it. And I have to work." He got a clean pot down from a hook and picked up a scouring pad.

"Bill, I'm not making any plans to send you back to Grandville, though I've thought of it. But I do want you to see a doctor."

He didn't want to go back to Grandville. He was not a crackminded old bean, he told himself. "I've got new teeth," he told her.

"I see," she said.

"I've got new teeth, so I don't want to see no doctor."

"I'm sorry, but you have to. Noon on Monday, okay?"

Bill gazed at the sink and listened as her footsteps crossed the room and went out through the door. His throat was clogged and his chest felt like it was being

83

crushed. He didn't want to see any doctor, and he didn't want to see Miss Keating anymore. He looked over at the door to be sure she was gone, then limped off to his room.

He had some money—a handful of coins—in the drawer by his bed. He gathered them all up and shuffled out the door. Past the kitchen and outside by the golf course there was a telephone booth. He closed himself into it and put one of the coins in the slot.

Karen, one of the waitresses who used to work in the coffee shop, always helped him dial the phone when he called Barry at the computer office. He tried to remember how she did it. He put his finger in one of the little holes and turned the dial. He continued turning the dial until a voice came on the receiver.

"You've reached a disconnected number. Can I help you?"

"I want to call Barry," he said.

"Do you have the number, sir?"

Bill stared at the phone, not knowing what to say.

"If you can give me the number, sir, perhaps I can help you."

"Number four," he said slowly, trying to remember any of the numbers he'd heard people say. "Four...five ...four, eight, seven, three, one...five."

"I'm afraid you have too many numbers."

Bill felt his throat tighten. He tried again. "One... four...eight, two, three, nine, six, seven."

"Sir," the lady said impatiently, "do you have the number written down?"

"I can remember," Bill said urgently. "I remember it. Four...six...one...two, five, five, five, two, two, seven, three, five, five." He swallowed hard and held his breath.

"Sir, unless you can give me the correct number, it's impossible to reach your party."

Bill stared silently at the telephone, his mind suddenly blank. Barry and Bev and Clay were somewhere very far away, and he didn't know the mysterious numbers that would let him talk to them. And Miss Keating was going to take him back to that terrible place on Monday. He slowly placed the receiver back on the hook. Then he limped aimlessly away, feeling a terrible tightness in his chest.

"I'm sorry I haven't had a chance to talk to you sooner," Tom Walz said to Barry. They were walking past the University library, under trees that were already turning to fall colors. "I hope you haven't had any serious problems. I mean aside from the usual chaos that characterizes a new year."

Tom Walz was a big, cheerful man with a wry sense of humor. From what Barry had observed, the other faculty members had a high regard for him. "None at all," Barry said. "We've got some gifted students here. They're all so eager to get their projects started they're stampeding me. They remind me of myself a couple years ago."

"Well, I'm supposed to begin my annual wrestling match with the Social Work department and the budget committee next week. So if there's anything special you need, let me know."

"There's a new compact video system out on the market," Barry said tentatively.

"Oh?"

"We could use it. I've already made a request for it."

Walz chuckled softly. "You did, huh? You're learning the game fast. Usually new instructors lay low for a year or two before they put the bite on me. Well, let's hear it."

Barry had brought along a copy of his request, anticipating a long battle to get what he needed. He handed Walz the paper.

Walz studied it and smiled. "Well, there goes the budget."

"We need it," Barry said.

"Okay, we'll see what we can do." He gave the

paper back. "By the way, I saw that unfinished film of yours the other day."

"The one on Bill Sackter?"

"Yes. That's what I wanted to talk to you about."

"Fine," Barry said. He was a little relieved. Everything was going fine in his classes, but when the boss wanted to have lunch, you never knew. And his interest in the Bill Sackter film sounded positive.

They had reached the faculty dining room, and Walz waited until they had ordered lunch before he returned to the subject. "It intrigued me how natural Bill was in front of the camera," he said. "You two must have had a good working relationship."

"Yes, we did. That was one of the things that kept me going. It turned out to be a labor of love. Sometimes I couldn't tell when the film ended and the friendship began."

"That's apparent in the film. The further along in the film the better he got. Where's Bill now?"

"Still working in the kitchen, I presume. I haven't talked to him for a while."

Their lunch came, and Walz buttered a roll. "It's interesting how so many states have adopted new programs to handle people like Bill. The programs seem to work out fine if the people are placed in situations where somebody really cares for them. But too often they end up in places where they're not wanted. Then it can be a lot worse than being in an institution. They can be very lonely."

Barry felt a pang of guilt, wondering if there was anybody at the country club taking any interest in Bill. He resolved to make a trip to Minneapolis as soon as possible. Or at least to call Bill.

A short, bearded man in his mid-fifties suddenly appeared at their table. He seemed to be irritated about something.

"Tom," he said, "I just saw my office assignment, and it's the size of a closet."

Walz gave him a disarming smile. "It's just an

experiment, Arthur. I'm trying to humanize this place a little."

The man was not mollified. "My secretary has a bigger office than I do!"

"And that's the point," Walz countered. "She has a more difficult workload and the pay is less. It's just normal—"

"What are you talking about?"

Walz smiled again. "Well, you teach two classes two days a week, right?"

"Yes. So?"

"So you've got it easy. She's got a much harder schedule to follow. Nine to five, and the rewards are less. So she deserves more office space."

The professor gaped at him. "Tom, what are you running here? Some kind of academic circus?"

"No. Just a more equitable distribution of office space based on workload. Give it a try, Arthur. And thanks for your cooperation."

The professor opened his mouth to protest, then thought better of it. He huffed and marched indignantly away.

Walz watched him go and chuckled. "The fewer the classes they teach, the larger the offices they want. If they only lectured an hour a week, they'd want a penthouse suite."

Thank God it was Friday, Barry reflected as he walked back to his classroom. All the tensions of the campus had eased, and half the students were lying on the grass contemplating the clouds. Barry felt like he was finally getting into the rhythmn of things, becoming a part of the "academic life."

He also felt good about Tom Walz's reaction to *The Bill Show*. It was the first time he'd let anybody see it, and his own feelings about it had been confirmed.

It was a beautiful Friday afternoon, but Barry's good feelings abruptly dissolved when he returned to his classroom. A pink telephone message was lying on his desk. At 1:25 P.M. a call had come from Miss Marge Keating at the welfare offices in Minneapolis. *Urgent,* the message said, *Please call back as soon as possible.*

Barry quickly strode to his office upstairs and called the number. There was only one possible reason for an urgent call from Miss Keating; something had happened to Bill.

"Do you remember me, Mr. Morrow?" Marge Keating said after he identified himself.

"Of course I remember you. What's the matter, Miss Keating?"

"Well, I called because I know you've had a special relationship with Bill Sackter. He's been in an accident."

Barry stopped breathing for an instant. "What kind of an accident? What happened?"

"It seems that he wandered off from the country club a couple of days ago. And then, last night, the State Police found him out in the countryside. Apparently he fell, or he was hit by a car."

"Oh, my God," Barry said. "How bad?"

"Well, no bones were broken. But he was unconscious, and his ulcerated leg was very bad. Apparently he'd been walking for a long time. The doctors are afraid they may have to amputate the leg."

"They can't do that," Barry exclaimed. "How can he work with only one leg?"

"He can't, of course. We'll have to send him back to Grandville."

Barry grimaced, remembering the basement ward, and Ray throwing his pegs around. "You can't do that, Miss Keating. What about his sister? Can't she take care of him?"

"Well, I'm trying to locate her. But so far I haven't had any luck."

Barry closed his eyes and rubbed his forehead, trying to calculate how soon he could be in Minneapolis if he got an early start tomorrow. "Listen, Miss Keating, I'll be up there tomorrow. What hospital is he in?"

"Union Memorial."

"I'll be there by noon. Don't do anything until I get there, okay?"

She sounded relieved. "That's fine, Mr. Morrow. I'll see you then."

Bev was concerned about Bill's condition, but she didn't understand the urgency of Barry's getting involved. "Maybe they can save the leg," she said, folding diapers on the couch. "And then he can just go back to the club. Maybe you're worrying about nothing, honey."

Barry had returned to his classroom, but had been too distracted to give the students his full attention. Now he paced the floor wondering if it would help if he drove up to Minneapolis tonight. "Miss Keating doesn't think it's very likely he'll be able to go back to the club. She thinks it's best to send him back to Grandville."

"Well," Bev said after a silence. "Maybe she's right."

Barry shoved his hands in his pockets and stared out the window. "No, she's wrong. I've seen that place, and it's really no good at all. It's exactly what Bill says it is—a hellhole. You slam the door on him and it's all over. His spirit'll be gone forever."

"Barry, I like Bill," Bev said in a measured tone. "You know I do. But...maybe you're giving him too much credit. Maybe he'll be happy—"

"Happy back there?" Barry snorted. "Content?"

"They're professionals, Barry. They know what's best."

"They may be professionals, but they're overworked and underpaid. Bill is just a number, a statistic to them. They've got a thousand others just like him. At best they can give him ten minutes of their time a week. And what does he do the rest of the time? He wanders around among wards full of screaming people. Most of them can't even talk. They're practically vegetables, Bev."

89

She sighed and stared at him. "What are you trying to say?"

"I want to go back," he said.

"You mean move back to Minneapolis?"

"Not necessarily. But I want to help him. I want to help him get settled somewhere. Maybe help find his sister...I don't know. But I want to do something."

"You're feeling guilty, aren't you?"

"Yes, I'm feeling guilty. I think I have good reason to."

She shook her head and set the diapers aside. "Barry, you've done all you can. You've done all anyone can expect. Why should you feel guilty? People get hit by cars, they die of cancer. You can't control those things. Forget about it, Barry. Please."

"Forget about Bill?"

"No, I don't mean forget about Bill. But you're not the only one concerned about him. There are the doctors, and Miss Keating, and all kinds of other people who are trained to deal with these problems."

"But I'm his friend, honey. I just want to give him some help. I want to make sure they don't take his leg off. I want to find his sister...do something for him."

"My brother's keeper," she said.

"And what's wrong with that?"

She took a deep breath and let it out. "And what if you don't find his sister? I mean, it's only been fifty years. Then what? Then what, Barry? Bring him back here, is that what you're thinking? You have a wife, a child...you've got responsibilities. Things are just getting going for us, and they're looking even better. Why do you want to mess it all up?"

Barry turned from the window and slouched into the big chair, thinking about all the months he'd spent with Bill. "I don't know what I want to do, but I have to do something, honey. I aimed a camera at this funny-looking old man, and I discovered something sweet and gentle in a person. He was not an idiot, or an imbecile, or some strange, emotionless specimen under a microscope. He was a human being. He was supposed to be remote and uncaring, but he wasn't. He has hopes and fears, and a lot more warmth than most people I've met.

"And what is life all about? Is the most important thing for me to be successful and make a lot of money so we can live in suburbia like my parents? So we can insulate ourselves from people like Bill? Or is it being human...caring and sharing with people like Bill? I just want to give him a chance. I thnk he's capable of making it in society, of being accepted, making it on his own. He just needs somebody to reach out and give him a hand. That's all I want to do, just help him out."

He wondered if he was making any sense. Bev didn't seem to think so. She silently gathered up the diapers and took them to the kitchen table.

"Bevie, I know we moved on, and things are going good, all of that. It's just that I don't want to leave something behind. I don't want to lose the ability to care...to be concerned about another human being. The least I can do is go up there and visit him in the hospital. I've got to do that, Bev."

She nodded, and then smiled warmly at him. "I know you do, honey. And whatever you decide, I know it will be the right thing."

X

Barry arrived at the Union Memorial Hospital at a quarter to twelve. William Sackter was on the third floor, the receptionist told him, and Barry caught an elevator just before it closed.

The third floor nurses scurried back and forth, their crisp uniforms rustling and their rubber-soled shoes squeaking on the polished linoleum. The place smelled of alcohol and antiseptic and mashed potatoes. Orderlies were working their way along the hall delivering lunches.

Barry tiptoed the last few steps to Bill's room and peered through the door. Bill was on the far side. He was sitting up in bed, but his chin was resting on his chest and he was staring glumly at his folded hands.

"Hey," Barry called out softly, "I'm looking for a regular good old man."

Bill's eyes widened and he stared, as if not believing what he saw. Then a big smile spread across his face. "Hi, buddy," he said and quickly reached up to straighten his wig. "Hi, buddy," he repeated, his voice cracking. "Hi, buddy!"

Barry strode across and embraced him. "Hi, buddy. How ya doin'?"

"I'm fine." He pounded Barry on the back. "I'm fine. Just fine. I'm glad to see you, Barry."

Barry drew back and glanced at the leg. It was bandaged heavily, only partially covered with the blanket. "I'm glad to see you, Bill."

"Did Sweetie come with you? And Clay?"

"No, they stayed home." Barry winked at him and chuckled. "I heard you went for a long walk."

Bill's face sagged and he lowered his head, as if ashamed of what he'd done. "I tried to call you, buddy," he said thickly. "The operator said she couldn't get you."

The thought struck Barry that Bill might have started walking to Iowa after the unsuccessful phone call. "I'm sorry, buddy. But I'm here now."

Bill nodded. "I'm glad to see you, buddy."

Miss Keating stuck her head in the door. "Hello, Bill," she called out.

Bill glanced at her, then scowled at his hands. "Hello."

Barry gave him a pat on the shoulder. "Listen, Bill. I want to talk to Miss Keating for a minute, but I'll be right back. Okay?"

"Don't let her send me to that place," Bill whimpered.

"Just take it easy," Barry said and walked out.

Miss Keating was standing a few paces down the hall, talking to a doctor. The man was about fifty; tall and gaunt with a weary look of resignation as he listened to Miss Keating.

"Mr. Morrow, this is Dr. Riis. He's been taking care of Bill."

The doctor smiled and shook his hand. "So you're the famous Barry Morrow. Bill talks about you all the time."

"Yeah," Barry said. "How bad is his leg?"

"Well, according to Bill, he's fine. Happy as a "lard." But the leg is pretty bad. He seems to be incapable of taking care of himself."

"That's my point exactly," Miss Keating agreed.

"It might have to come off," Riis said. "And Miss Keating was just telling me that Bill may have to go back to an institution."

"What are the chances of saving the leg?"

The doctor sighed. "There's a fairly good chance we can save it. But that's not the whole problem. The ulcerations are very susceptible to infection, and the leg has to be bathed every day and kept clean. Apparently Bill just isn't capable of doing that. So whether we take it off or leave it on, he's going to have to have somebody looking after him. Which I presume means he goes back to the institution."

"Yeah, that would be the easiest thing," Barry said with a touch of sarcasm.

Miss Keating gave him a hard look. "Do you have a better idea, Mr. Morrow?"

Barry sympathized with her frustration. She probably had dozens of other people like Bill to look after, and the Welfare Department was not about to hire around-the-clock nurses for them. "What about his sister? Did you find her?"

"Yes, she's living in Tampa. But she's an invalid in a nursing home, incapable of taking him."

Barry took a deep breath, hoping he would not regret what he was about to do. "What if I took Bill home with me?"

Miss Keating stared at him. "To Iowa?"

Barry nodded. "To Iowa."

"Well," she said, suddenly becoming a bureaucrat again. "That would be difficult."

"Why?"

"Well..." She hesitated, then softened, allowing herself a smile. "It would be difficult. The Welfare Department is involved. But I think it could be done."

"Okay, let's do it," Barry said.

Miss Keating was doubtful. "Are you certain you want to do this, Mr. Morrow?"

Until he'd walked into Bill's room, Barry hadn't been certain about anything. Now he had no doubts. "Yes," he said.

"All right," she agreed.

Dr. Riis smiled, suddenly not so weary anymore. "I'm sure we can save that leg, Mr. Morrow."

Barry grinned and walked back to Bill's door. "Hey, buddy," he called out, "we're going to Iowa."

Bill gaped at him.

"You and me, buddy, we're going to Iowa," Barry repeated.

Bill's eyes glistened and a big smile brightened his face. "You and me, buddy," he said throatily, "we're goin' to I-O-way."

On Monday morning Bill was released from the hospital, and Barry drove him to the country club to pick up his gear. They found a couple of empty cartons in the kitchen, and Bill threw his things into them like a condemned prisoner who'd gotten a last-minute reprieve.

"You understand what the Welfare Department said, don't you?" Barry asked as he repacked the clothes more neatly.

"Sure, we're goin' to I-O-way," Bill answered.

94

"Yeah, but it's a trial set-up, and I'm going to be your guardian as long as everything works out. We have to find you a nice place to live, a good job, and integrate you into society. Right?"

Bill nodded and jammed his hats into one of the boxes. "Right, we're gonna innegrate ol' Bill. Everything's gonna be okey-dokey."

"And you've got to take care of that leg."

"Take care of the leg," Bill echoed.

Barry pulled a piece of paper from his jacket pocket. "And I want you to have this."

"What is that?"

"It's a piece of paper from the Welfare Department."

Bill took it and frowned at the unintelligible words. "What's it say?"

"It says you're on your own now."

"It says that?"

"Right there." Barry pointed at the top of the paper. "It says, 'Tell everyone that Bill Sackter is a regular good man, and he's now on his own.'"

Bill happily rocked his head from side to side and folded the paper. "That's good," he said. "I'll keep this."

"It's yours."

"I'll put it in my wallet next to my two-dollar bill. My lucky two-dollar bill. I don't want to lose it." He stuffed the paper in his wallet and put the wallet carefully back in his pocket. "Ol' Bill is on his own now."

"How's your leg?"

"It's fine."

"Then let's get out of here."

"Yeah. Don't forget my TV set."

"I won't forget your TV set."

The paper saying Bill was on his own was not quite as simple as Barry had described it. As enthusiastic as Marge Keating was about Barry's taking Bill to Iowa, her boss had taken a dimmer view of the idea, and on

Saturday afternoon Barry had spent three hours in the welfare offices getting a final approval for the move.

"I appreciate your altruistic motives in all this Mr. Morrow," the Director said. "It is certainly an admirable gesture."

"It's more than a gesture, Mr. Kroehler," Barry told him.

Kroehler was in his mid-sixties, a big man who might once have been a defensive tackle for the Minnesota Vikings. He creaked back and forth in his leather chair, eyeing Barry as if he were a spectator at a football game who had come down out of the stands and volunteered to substitute for an injured quarterback.

"I'm sure it is," he said. "But I also wonder if you're asking to take on a burden you may not fully understand. Miss Keating tells me you've been his friend for some time now, and that you've been making some kind of documentary film about him."

"That's true," Barry answered. "But the film was certainly secondary. At least it was after I got to know Bill. As a matter of fact I set the film aside some time ago."

"I see. But you have to appreciate that being Bill's friend and visiting him two or three times a week, is quite a different thing from being responsible for him every minute of his life. It's like adopting a child who can't take care of himself. Are you prepared to take care of him when he gets sick? Or when he wanders off somewhere? Or if he doesn't like his job, or doesn't like where he's living?"

Barry really didn't anticipate any serious problems like that. "I think so," he said.

The Director gazed coolly at him. "Thinking so may not be good enough, Mr. Morrow. As well as you and Bill get along with each other, these things will happen. Anything that can happen to a five-year-old child can happen to Bill. It's dangerous for him to cross a busy street by himself. It's dangerous for him to do a lot of things."

"But I think he's capable of learning how to do a lot of these things safely," Barry countered.

"Of course he is. But that's my point in a way. Teaching him such things is very time consuming. Do you really have the time? Do you have the time to watch over him when he's sick, or help him when he's unhappy about his job or his living conditions, or his social life?"

It seemed to Barry that he could certainly give Bill as much time as the Welfare Department had given him. "I'm sure I'll have enough time to give him a better life than he would have in Grandville."

There was no way the Director could refute that. He nodded and let it pass. "But if, in a month, or six months, you decide that Bill is too big a burden for you, and you change your mind about all this, we're going to have a very serious problem on our hands, Mr. Morrow. It could be devastating for someone like Bill."

Barry was about to say he didn't "think" that would happen. But the Director had already pointed out that "thinking" such things was not good enough. "It won't happen," he said firmly.

The Director gazed silently at him for a minute, then sat forward. "I hope you're right. Now, I think you can understand that this is a very serious action for us to take. If things should turn out badly, this department will ultimately have to accept the responsibility. So we're going to require weekly reports through the first three months, and then periodic reports after that. We will also require that Bill's housing situation be approved by either a state or county government authority in Iowa. The same for his work situation. Also, we will require medical reports." He looked questioningly at Barry. "I understand you're teaching at the University there. Is that correct?"

"Yes."

"I see. Well, perhaps you can make some arrangements to have the University medical staff look at Bill's leg."

"I'll try to work that out," Barry said.

Kroehler nodded. "All right, Mr. Morrow. I'm going to approve this, but only because you're not taking Bill very far away. Under no circumstances can you take him out of Iowa, except to return him to Minnesota. Is that understood?"

"Yes. That'll be no problem."

"Very well." Kroehler rose and held out his hand. He smiled, but not very enthusiatscally. "I wish you the best of luck, and I hope you know what you're getting into."

With Marge Keating's help, Barry had spent the rest of the afternoon filling out forms attesting to the fact that he was not a white-slaver, a communist, a sexual deviate, or an alien from Mars bent on destroying the world. Then he had walked out with five pounds of blank "weekly report" forms, and three copies of the official document saying Bill was now his responsibility.

Leaving the hospital, collecting his things at the country club and driving to Iowa was probably the happiest day of Bill's life. He sat in the car with his wig perched on his head and smiled out at the passing scenery like a man who was seeing trees and cows and farmhouses and wheat fields for the first time in his life.

Barry felt almost as good, but he waited until they crossed the Iowa border and reached Charles City before he made the phone call he'd been putting off for almost forty-eight hours.

"Did they have to operate on the leg?" Bev asked.

Barry had decided not to tell her about his big decision until Dr. Riis had given the final word on Bill, and that had not come until Sunday night. "No," he said. "Apparently the antibiotics took care of it. The doctor said he seems to be making a miraculous recovery."

"That's marvelous. When are you coming home?"

"I'll be there in about three hours. And Bev... you know that conversation we had before I left..."

"Don't say another word," she broke in. "Bill's with you, isn't he?"

"Yes."

"It's okay," she said. "It's the only thing you could do." She laughed happily. "I guess that's why I married Barry Morrow in the first place."

Barry hadn't realized how much the tension had been building in him. Now it suddenly dissolved. "Bev, you're great. I love you."

"You're not such a bad guy yourself," she said. "Hurry home."

Barry hung up and came grinning back to the car. "Let's get ourselves a sensational lunch, Bill."

"Okay, buddy," Bill said. "That sounds good. I'm hungry."

"How about thirty-one pieces of chicken?"

"Okay. Good. Yeah! Thirty-one pieces of chicken!"

Bev was waiting at the top of the stairs when they got home. "I'm so glad to see you," she bubbled. "Is that old Bill? Is that old Wild Bill from Borneo?"

"It's me," Bill said hobbling up the steps. "I'm here."

"Welcome to Iowa, Bill."

He huffed and puffed a little, but grinned all the way up. "I like I-O-way," he said. "Everything's nice here."

Barry struggled up the steps behind him, carrying the boxes.

Bill wanted to see Clay, who was having his nap. He stood beside the crib and smiled at him as if he'd found another lost friend.

"Tom Walz called a few minutes ago," Bev said when they returned to the living room. "He said you called him last night."

"Yeah. I told him to get a substitute for me today."

"He said if you brought Bill home, he thought he might have some work for him. He wants you to bring Bill to his office before your first class tomorrow."

That was the best news Barry had heard all day. The thought of spending hours on the phone trying to find some kind of work for Bill was a chore he hadn't been looking forward to.

After dinner, Barry took Bill into the bathroom where they washed his leg according to the doctor's instructions, and he tried to impress on Bill that he must do it at least every day. Bill solemnly agreed, saying he didn't want to lose the leg and have to go back to Grandville. Then he put on his pajamas and fell asleep, smiling peacefully in front of the television set.

"Do you think it's going to work?" Bev asked after they got Bill settled in Clay's room and went to bed.

Barry hadn't thought about anything beyond the task of getting Bill to Iowa. Whatever new problems arose, he would deal with them as they came along, he had decided. "It'll work," he said confidently.

XI

Bill liked the campus. He smiled happily at all the students scurrying to make their eight o'clock classes. "There are lots of young people here," he said.

"Yeah, lots of young people."

Bill had insisted on wearing his wig, and some of the students who weren't too preoccupied to notice, gave him startled glances and then hurried on, grinning.

Tom Walz's office was on the third floor, and his secretary ushered them straight in. The room was cluttered with books and file cabinets. He rose and came around his desk beaming. "Hi, Bill, I'm Tom Walz," he said with his hand extended. "That's Thomas, Tom for short," he added.

Bill warmed to him immediately. "William, Bill for short," he answered.

"Sit down, sit down. I've been looking forward to

meeting you, Bill. I've seen your movie, *The Bill Show*, and I feel like we're old friends."

Bill nodded happily. "*The Bill Show*. That's a good one."

"It certainly is. Now, I understand you're looking for a job. I think I may have just the thing for you. Do you like working outside?"

Bill seemed a little confused. "I worked in the kitchen before."

"Well, maybe we can find something like that for you later. But right now I can get you a job with the maintenance department." He glanced at Barry. "Ed Jenkins runs the department, and he's an old friend. I talked to him about you, Bill, and he said he'd like to have you working for him. It'll be raking leaves and dong some clean-up work, and maybe some scraping and painting. Would you like that?"

Bill nodded. "I'm a good scraper," he said. "I can do all those things."

Barry smiled to himself. Bill probably held the world's record for scraping pots and pans.

"Okay," Tom said. "I'll take you over and introduce you to Ed this morning. And now, I understand you're looking for a place to live."

It was all coming too fast for Bill. He nodded uncertainly.

"Well, there's a room for rent at a house out on Taylor Street, only a short bus ride from the campus. A woman named Mae Driscoll runs it, and she'll be happy to take you in. She's very nice, and it's a good, clean place. So I'll give the address to Barry, and maybe he can take you over there this afternoon to take a look."

Bill fidgeted and glanced at Barry. "I'm living with Barry and Bev and Clay right now," he said. "I like it there."

"That's okay," Barry said quickly. "We'll just go over and have a look at the house. If you don't like it, we'll look for something else."

"Okay," Bill murmured uncertainly.

Barry glanced at his watch and rose. "Well, I'd better get going. I've got a nine o'clock class."

A sudden look of panic came to Bill's face, but Tom Walz quickly defused it. "Fine. Bill and I'll just stay here and talk about *The Bill Show* for a minute. Then I'll take him over and meet Ed."

"I'll see you later, buddy," Barry said.

"Okay, see you later, buddy," Bill answered.

Tom Walz walked Barry to the door. "Mae Driscoll has one other boarder like Bill," he said quietly when they were outside. "I think it might be a good spot for him."

"Thanks, Tom. You're solving a lot of problems for me."

"That's my job," he said with a laugh. "I keep my faculty members free from worries so they can do their best for their students. Just don't ask me for a bigger office." He started back into the office, then stopped short. "Oh, by the way, don't mention Bill's job to anybody around here. It's kind of an unofficial arrangement I've made with Ed Jenkins. The administration wouldn't be happy if they knew about it."

"Why not?" Barry asked.

"Well, they've got pretty strict hiring requirements around here. Civil service kind of exams, and all that sort of thing. But don't worry about it."

After his eleven o'clock class, Barry found Bill at the far end of the campus, scraping old paint off of a steel bannister. He seemed to be enjoying himself, attacking the railing with the same vigor he used to have cleaning pots and pans. His boss, Ed Jenkins, was watching him from a distance, chewing on a cigar butt. Jenkins was a stubby little man with gray whiskers and an elfinlike face. Barry introduced himself.

"He's a nice old guy," Jenkins said. "But does he always wear that crazy toupee?"

Barry told him about Bill's theory of a "regular good man" having a full head of hair.

"An interesting idea," Jenkins said. "But he sticks out like a sore thumb. And I'm supposed to keep it quiet that I've hired him. It's like having one of the Three Stooges on my crew and expecting nobody to notice."

Barry took Bill to lunch, and finally persuaded him to wear a hat when he came to work the next day. Then he delivered him back to Ed Jenkins, feeling pleased with the way things had worked out. At five o'clock he picked Bill up again and they drove to Mae Driscoll's boarding house on Taylor Street.

It was a neat-looking white frame house with a big elm tree in front and a rose-covered picket fence running around the yard. The neighborhood around it seemed to be in a state of transition. Mixed with the older homes were a good number of fancy new suburban estates.

Bill stared uneasily at the place. "Maybe we could come back tomorrow," he said.

"I've already called her, Bill. She's expecting us."

Bill sank lower in the seat. "Maybe you could call her again tomorrow. And we better get home for dinner."

Barry shook his head. "On your own, that was the deal, Bill. Remember? I think you'll like her. She sounded very nice on the telephone."

Bill looked at the house again, and Barry circled the car and opened his door. As if he were marching off to the executioner, Bill slid out of the seat and slowly followed Barry through the front gate. Before Barry could press the bell, the door opened.

"Hello, Mr. Morrow," the woman said and smiled at Bill. "And you must be Bill."

She was a plump, white-haired woman in her sixties. Except for the way she was dressed, she might have looked like everybody's favorite grandmother. She was wearing a faded pink blouse, a purple sweater and bright green slacks. Her blouse was buttoned in the wrong holes, Barry noticed, and half of her collar flopped too far over the sweater. But her questionable taste in fashions was more than made up for by her jolly manner.

"Come on in," she said. "I've got coffee ready, and your room's all been repainted." She closed the door behind them and gestured broadly to the side. "That's the living room. Color TV and lots of soft chairs. Your room will be up these stairs."

The living room looked like it had been furnished in the twenties. The mohair sofa and chairs were draped with lace antimacassars, and the lamps had tassels dangling from the shades.

Bill was a little taken aback by the woman's flamboyant dress and manner. He followed her silently up the stairs. At the top they turned back toward the front of the house.

"Here we are," she said and led them into the bedroom.

It was good-sized, and all freshly painted, with cheerfully colored curtains, bedspreads and chairs. Two big windows looked out at the elm tree, and the late afternoon sun poured into the room. On either side of the windows were an assortment of healthy-looking plants.

Bill gawked at everything, obviously impressed. "You take care of all them plants?" he asked.

"Yes, I do," she said.

Bill nodded. "That's nice."

"Are you a religious man, Bill?" she asked.

The answer surprised Barry. He had never discussed anything as abstract as religion with Bill. "Yes," he said.

"That's nice," Mae responded. "What affiliation?"

"Oh, I like all churches and temples," he said. "'Cause then I can speak to the Lord."

"Well, that's just wonderful," she said. "I've always said that a person needs two things to be happy in life: a good church and a good friend."

Bill nodded emphatically. "If you have a good friend like Barry, then you're not a crackminded old man."

"My sentiments exactly," Mae said. "Now, let's go have some coffee."

"What do you think, Bill?" Barry asked as Mae left them alone.

Bill nodded. "I like it here." He turned a complete circle and gave every part of the room a second look. "I like it here," he said again.

Barry grinned. "Okay, let's go have a cup of coffee."

A man and a woman were sitting at the kitchen table, both in their mid-fifties. The woman was dressed in a frilly pink dress, and her hair was done in Shirley Temple curls. The man was wearing overalls and looked a little more sensible.

"Angela and Kenny," Mae said. "this is Bill Sackter and Barry Morrow. Bill is coming to live with us."

Kenny rose and timidly stuck out a hand, but Angela squinted suspiciously at Bill. "You have funny hair," she said.

"Now, Angela," Mae said, "that's not a nice thing to say to our new friend. Bill has very nice hair."

Angela tightened her mouth and lifted a Raggedy Ann doll from her lap. She sat it on the table in front of her and said harshly: "Now, you be a good girl and don't say bad things to Bill."

Bill didn't appear to be upset. He sat down and smiled at Kenny and Angela. "This is a nice place. I like it here."

"Kenny is our handyman around the house," Mae said as she poured coffee. "He can fix anything."

Kenny was a tall bony man with straight shoulders and a shrinking manner, as if he was trying to hide himself behind the table. He pulled himself awkwardly to his feet. "Well, I guess I'd better go to my room," he said and hurried out.

"Kenny's shy," Angela snickered. She tossed her head, and her dangling curls bounced and jiggled. "He's afraid of everything."

"That's not true," Mae said firmly.

"Yes it is. He's shy, shy, shy. Goodbye." Angela

jumped to her feet, and holding up the Raggedy Ann doll as a partner, waltzed happily out of the room.

Bill seemed indifferent to the strange behavior. It occurred to Barry that the old man had spent most of his life surrounded by people in a lot worse shape than Mae, Kenny and Angela. At least they could talk and take care of themselves.

"I presume your boardinghouse is approved by the county, Mrs. Driscoll?" Barry said.

"Oh, yes," she assured him. "But I'll have to tell them about Bill. They'll probably want to come out and take a look at the arrangements, but I'm sure everything will be all right."

"Then I think everything's fine. What do you think, Bill?"

"Everything's fine," Bill said. "Hunky-dory." He nodded and grinned.

After work the next day, Barry helped Bill move his things into Mae's boardinghouse and Bill became an official member of the family. While they carried boxes upstairs, Angela continued to taunt Bill about his hair and the way he limped when he walked. But Bill handled the situation very well. Instead of responding to the insults, he adopted Mae's manner and told Angela it was not nice to speak to people that way. Just as she had done in the kitchen. Angela huffed and squirmed and passed on the advice to her doll.

Once Bill was moved in, Barry showed him how he could walk from the boardinghouse to the bus stop, and then let him try it on his own. Bill successfully negotiated only one of the four blocks before he made a wrong turn. He had learned to count well enough that he could sit down and number all of his fingers. But when he started walking, his mind drifted. By the time he reached the end of the first block, he couldn't remember how far he'd gone.

Barry took him back to the house and started over again, urging him to concentrate. On the second trip he made it through two blocks before the system broke down. Instead of turning, he continued straight. So Barry picked him up and drove him to work the next day, and they practiced the walking routine every night for the rest of the week.

By Friday Bill could make it confidently through three blocks. At that point he could see the bus stop ahead, and could finish up by dead reckoning navigation. To celebrate, Barry brought him home for dinner, and Bill proudly described his accomplishments to Clay and Bev. He was now a first-class regular man who knew how to walk all the way from his house to the bus stop without getting lost.

Mae Driscoll was a very good cook, he told Barry and Bev. Angela Pirkle was a little bit crackminded, because she had a doll that she thought was a baby. Sometimes Angela was mean to him, and he got mad at her. But he was trying to help her because Angela didn't have a friend, and he felt sorry for her. But he liked Kenny very much, because Kenny was not crackminded. Kenny was just shy, and he hardly ever went out of the house. Bill was going to try to teach him how to walk over to the bus stop, the same as he did.

Everything was turning out wonderfully, Barry decided, as he drove Bill home that night and watched him shuffle through the gate and disappear into his new home. Bill had a job, he liked where he was living, and he had taken it upon himself to help Kenny overcome his shyness. It looked like he was well on his way to becoming a "regular first-class man."

XII

By the middle of the second week Bill had finished scraping all of the bannisters. He was good at it. He could scrape away the old paint right down to the metal and make it all shiny in the sunlight, and he could even dig into the cracks and crevices and make them clean and smooth too. He was a regular first-class scraper, and a lot of the students stopped on their way to classes and talked to him and told him what a good job he was doing.

Ed Jenkins thought so too, and the next morning he brought Bill a can of dull red paint and showed him how to dip a brush into the can and spread the paint over the metal. "This is primer," Ed told him. "Now, you don't have to put it on thick, but you gotta be sure all the metal is covered. Okay, now you hold the brush like this."

Bill couldn't wait to try it. He took the brush and dipped it into the paint can and moved the brush back and forth over the metal. But the paint dribbled from the brush and dripped on the concrete steps and ran down his fingers and hand.

Ed Jenkins laughed. Then he relighted his little cigar butt and showed Bill how to scrape the brush across the edge of the can before he spread the paint on the metal. But Bill still couldn't get the hang of it. Even before he lifted the brush to the bannister, the paint oozed across his hand again, and some of it splattered on his shoes. He put the brush back in the can, stood up and backed away. "I don't like to paint," he said.

Ed Jenkins laughed again. "That's okay, Bill. I'll get somebody else to do this. Come on with me."

Bill shuffled along behind him, feeling embarrassed by his failure. "I'm a good scraper," he said.

"You're a great scraper," Ed Jenkins answered. "You're the best scraper I've ever seen. But we don't have anything more to scrape."

Bill wondered if Ed Jenkins was going to tell him to go home. If he didn't have a job anymore, Barry would be mad. Then he might send him back to Minneapolis and Miss Keating.

Ed Jenkins turned and slapped him on the shoulder. "Hey, don't look so glum, pal. How good are you with a broom? You ever done any sweeping?"

"I'm a good sweeper," Bill answered. "I'm a real good sweeper." He had swept out the kitchen at the country club lots of times. And before that he had worked in a big warehouse where he swept the whole thing every day. "I'm a good sweeper," he said again.

They had reached the maintenance building and Ed Jenkins picked up a wide broom and headed out across the grass toward a big building covered with vines. "They got a little playground over here for kids," he said. "They got classrooms with a couple dozen preschoolers they use for new teaching ideas and stuff. So we gotta keep the place cleaned up. You like kids?"

Bill nodded, trying to keep up with Ed's fast strides. "I like kids. Barry and Bev have a kid. His name is Clay."

"That so? Well, while the kids are in class, you can sweep up the playground. Then after they go home this afternoon, you can sweep out the classroom. That sound okay?"

"Okay," Bill said. "That sounds hunky-dory."

"Okay, hunky-dory." Ed stopped at the edge of the playground. "This is it. There's a couple of trash barrels over there by the building. So just sweep up all these leaves and put 'em in the barrels. If you get that done before the kids go home, then you can sweep off those walks along the side of the building. Okay?"

"I can do that. Sure. I can do that okay."

"Good. If you have any questions, ask Florence Archer. She's the teacher. So if this works out, we'll just make this your permanent job—keepin' this whole area swept and cleaned up. How about it?"

"That's good," Bill agreed. "I'd like that."

"Okay, pal. I'll bring your lunch over at noon."

Ed Jenkins walked away puffing his cigar and Bill surveyed the playground. There were slides and swings, and a big dome-shaped thing made out of steel bars for

109

the kids to climb on. There was also a big sandbox and some little toy cars for the kids to ride on.

Bill had a dim recollection of playing in the sand when he was a little boy. And once he had gotten on a swing and swung back and forth so high it was like flying in an airplane. He gazed idly at the swings for a long time, then he remembered the sweeping. There were a lot of dead leaves lying around, and Ed wanted them all put into the trash barrels.

He had swept the first pile of leaves over to the trash barrels and was scooping them in when the classroom door opened and all the children came running out. Bill stopped working and watched.

They yelled and laughed and raced each other to the slides and swings. Some of them threw balls back and forth, and others rode the little cars around and bumped into each other. Behind them, a tall slender woman with glasses stood by the classroom door watching.

Bill finished loading the trash barrel, then carried his broom around the edge of the playground, wondering if he was supposed to continue sweeping while the children were playing. Over by the swings on the far side, a little girl was sitting on a bench all by herself. She was a pretty little girl with reddish brown hair, and she was all buttoned up in a brown coat. Her face was pale and she looked lonesome.

Bill continued around the playground until he reached the bench. It would be hard to sweep with all the children running around and playing on the swings. He could ask the teacher about it, but she had gone back into the classroom. He sat down and smiled at the little girl.

"Hi," she said and smiled back at him.

"Hi," Bill answered.

"What's your name?"

"William. Bill for short. Bill." He waited for her to stick out her hand, but she kept them both deep in her coat pockets.

"My name is Amy," she said. "Where do you live?"

"I live at Mae's house. Where do you live?"

"With my mommy. Why are you wearing a cowboy hat?"

Bill had forgotten which hat he was wearing today. He reached up and made sure it was on straight. "I like hats," he said. "I've got lots of hats."

She stared at him, then kicked her dangling feet back and forth. "I've got a cat. Her name is Shana."

Bill liked the name. "That's a good name. I never had a cat." He remembered his harmonica and fished it out of his pocket.

"What's that?" she asked.

"It's a harmonica. I'll play it for you." He played "She'll Be Coming Around the Mountain," stamping his foot to the rhythm. Amy's eyes widened and she grinned and kicked her feet back and forth. When he finished, three or four other children had moved closer to watch. Amy stared hard at the harmonica as if it had magically produced the music all by itself. "Where did you get that?" she asked.

"In a store. I got two more at Mae's house."

A bell rang and the teacher suddenly appeared outside the door again. All the children except Amy trudged away.

"Play it again," she said.

Bill lifted the harmonica to his mouth, then stopped short as the teacher called out.

"Amy! Come along now!"

Amy glanced at the teacher and sighed. "I guess I have to go." She jumped down from the bench.

The teacher met her halfway to the door and took her hand. "You shouldn't talk to strangers, dear," she said.

"He's not a stranger, Miss Archer. "He's Bill."

The teacher frowned curiously at Bill and then closed the door as they disappeared inside.

Amy was a nice little girl, Bill decided, as he picked up his broom and went back to work.

Once all the problems with Bill were squared away, Barry plunged himself back into work. In the four classes he taught, he had a total of eighty-six students. Each of them had a film or videotape project going, for which each of them wanted advice, counseling and technical help. Barry found himself staying up till midnight every night looking at tapes and films, and on weekends he had little time to spend with Bev and Clay, much less with Bill. In the following weeks he occasionally saw Bill on campus, and he talked to him several times on the phone.

Everything seemed to be "hunky-dory" with Bill. But one day when Barry had some free time and he set out to find the old man and take him to lunch, he suddenly found that Bill had vanished.

The last time he'd seen him Bill had been sweeping leaves in the preschool play yard. Bill liked children, and it seemed like a good spot for him. When Barry arrived, the kids were all sitting on the benches eating their lunches, but Bill was nowhere in sight. Barry continued on around the building and across the grass to the maintenance department. Ed Jenkins was at the back of the building, helping two men unload roofing materials from a truck.

"Hi, Barry," Jenkins said, "where's your friend today?"

It was the same question Barry had been about to ask. "What do you mean? Isn't he here?"

"Nope. He didn't show up this morning. I figured he was sick or something. I guess he doesn't know how to use a phone, huh?"

There was no reason to be alarmed, Barry told himself. But he still felt a small vacuum in his stomach. "Yeah, that's probably it. If he shows up, tell him I was looking for him."

"Right," Jenkins said and smiled. "Tell him we miss him."

Where was a telephone? Barry hurried back across the grass and strode up the steps into the Social Work building. There was a booth just inside the door. He found a dime and dialed the boardinghouse.

"Mae, this is Barry Morrow. Is Bill there?"

"Bill? No, he went to work today. He left at the usual time: seven-thirty."

Barry took a reinforcing breath. "And you haven't seen him since?"

"No. Why? Is something wrong?"

"He didn't show up for work, Mae. He hasn't been here all day."

"Oh, my! Where could he be?"

God only knows, Barry thought. "Listen, could you go out and see if he's wandering around the neighborhood somewhere? I'll be right over."

"All right. I'll get Angela to help me."

Barry hung up and tried to think. Had Bill gotten lost before he reached the bus stop? Or had he gotten off the bus at the wrong place? Or had he gotten lost after he reached the campus? Any one of them was a possibility.

He called Tom Walz and explained the situation.

"Don't worry about this end," Tom said. "I'll alert all the campus security guards and have them search every corner of the place. And forget your afternoon classes. I'll find somebody to fill in for you if you're not back."

"Thanks, Tom."

"You think you should call the city police?"

"Well . . . not yet. Let me cruise around for a while first."

Barry hung up and felt a pang of guilt over missing classes. This was the third time he'd asked Tom to cover for him since he'd started. It was not a good beginning for a new teacher.

He drove slowly along the bus route, looking carefully at every short man standing on a corner or walking along the street. Bill had been missing for more than five hours now. Where would he go? The last time he'd gone for a long walk in Minneapolis he had probably been headed for Iowa. What might he have in mind this time? Or was he just wandering?

On the off chance that he might have gone to see

113

Bev and Clay, Barry pulled into a gas station and called home.

"No, he hasn't been here," Bev told him. "Do you think he might have been in an accident?"

"No. He has identification in his wallet. They'd have called the house if he was hurt. Don't worry about it, I'll find him."

He found Mae and Angela walking along the street two blocks from the house. They hadn't seen Bill.

"Bill forgot his lunch this morning," Angela said. "He forgets his lunch all the time." She delivered the news with a smug smile and clutched her Raggedy Ann.

Mae and Angela climbed in the car. "What happens when he forgets his lunch?" Barry asked. "Does he come back home?"

"No," Mae said. "I usually send Angela after him with it. But I didn't notice until it was too late this morning. Oh, my, what'll we do?"

"Just drive around for a while," Barry said. "Are there any parks nearby?"

They made a tour of all the parks, with no luck. Barry didn't know whether to be angry or alarmed. On that first day Bill had moved into Mae's house, Barry had given him a card with Mae's address and telephone number and instructed him that any time he got lost he should show the card to someone and ask them to dial Mae's number for him. But he had probably forgotten. Or maybe he was having a good time somewhere.

It was three-thirty in the afternoon before Barry decided to give up and call the police. He hated to do it, because Bill felt the same way about policemen as he did about Grandville. But there was no other way.

Mae started making coffee as soon as they got back to the house, and Barry looked up the number of the police. He was dialing when Kenny came hesitantly into the kitchen.

"Somebody called while you were gone," he said.

Barry stopped dialing. "Who?"

"Uh . . . the Police Department. They said they have Bill there."

"Oh, thank the Lord," Mae exclaimed.

Angela snickered. "Bill's been arrested. Bill's been bad. He's going to jail."

"Did they say which police station?" Barry asked.

"They said he was downtown, and they would keep him until you came and got him."

Except for the clicking of typewriters and an occasional phone ringing, the police station was quiet. A white-haired sergeant led Barry to a small interrogation room in the rear. "We picked him up," he said. "He didn't look like the usual wino, but he was passing around the bottle with the regulars. Is he a mental case?"

"No," Barry said. "He's retarded, but he's not psychopathic."

"Yeah . . . well, he came along quietly. He's been dozing ever since we brought him in."

"Was he drunk?"

The sergeant waggled a hand. "A little tipsy, but not overboard. I think he's probably slept it off by now." He pushed open the door.

Bill was sitting in a straight-backed chair, his chin resting on his chest, half asleep. His lips were moving as if he was talking to himself.

"Hi, Bill," Barry said quietly.

The old man looked up and blinked, his face contorted as if he were going to cry. "I got lost, Barry," he whimpered. "I got lost."

The sergeant left them alone and Barry sat down. "Are you okay?"

"I'm okay. But I got lost. I forgot my lunch."

"So you went back to the house?"

Bill nodded and sniffled back the tears. "But I got lost."

"It's okay. You're found now. But why didn't you show somebody that card I gave you?"

Bill frowned as if he'd never heard of such a thing. Then it came to him. "Oh, yeah. I forgot."

Barry sighed and leaned forward on the desk. "This isn't working out very well, is it, Bill? You're supposed to be on your own now, and you're supposed to remember things like that card."

"I forgot," he said again.

"I know you forgot. And when you forget, I have to leave my work and come looking for you. If I have to do that too many times I'll lose my job, Bill. How did you end up with a bottle of wine?"

"I din't have a bottle of wine. Al gave it to me. Al is a good regular man."

"I don't think Al is a good regular man. Did you give Al any money?"

Bill nodded as if proud of himself. "I gave him my money, and he told me to stick with him. He said we were buddies, and we could have a good time together."

"Terrific," Barry said dryly. "Okay, let's go home."

Bill slowly pulled himself up and limped to the door, grimacing with each step.

"You're leg hurting?"

"It's okay."

Barry walked him down the corridor. "Have you been washing it every day?"

Bill shrugged. "I'm all alone," he whimpered.

"What does that have to do with it?"

"I don't like Angela anymore."

Barry was getting a little tired of the *non sequiturs*. "When was the last time you cleaned your leg, Bill?"

He was on the verge of crying again. "I don't know." He held onto Barry's arm going down the steps, then hung his head and shuffled to the car.

"I don't know what I'm going to do with you, Bill," Barry said and opened the door for him.

"I'm just a crackminded old man," he mumbled.

"You're not a crackminded old man!" Barry slammed the door and went around to the driver's side. Bill was slouched in the seat, staring at his hands.

"What do you think we ought to do?" Barry asked as he drove to the house. "You didn't show up for work today, you gave all your money to some guy, then you sat around drinking wine all day. And you haven't been keeping your leg clean. What should I do with you?"

He shrugged. "Throw me away. Ol' Bill's just no good."

"Stop saying that. I want you to think about it, Bill. We've got to figure out something, because it can't go on like this. I can't be with you all the time, and you've got to take care of yourself."

"I'm sorry," he whimpered.

Barry dropped it and drove on, remembering Kroehler's warnings about all the demands Bill might make on his time. Maybe Kroehler was right, and he'd bitten off more than he could chew. But there was nothing he could do about it now. And what other choice was there: to let Bill go back to Grandville? No, he had to make it work.

When they walked in the house, Angela was standing in the hall, clutching her doll and smirking. "You've been bad," she said. "You're going to have to stay in jail for a long time."

"Stop it, Angela," Barry said. "Bill has not been bad, and he's not going to jail. Where's Mae?"

"She's in the kitchen making dinner."

Bill hung his head and climbed the stairs. Barry followed him to his room. "Get your pants off, Bill, and let's go in the bathroom and get your leg cleaned up. Then we'd better have the doctor look at it tomorrow."

Bill did as he was told, and sat on the edge of the bathtub while Barry washed his leg. It was red and puffy and some of the sores were running again. Bill frowned at the leg as if he had never seen it before.

"You've got to do this every morning Bill. And it wouldn't hurt to do it again at night."

"I forgot," he mumbled.

Mae came through the open door and smiled at Bill. "Well, we're certainly glad to see you. Are you all right?"

"I'm fine," Bill answered.

"You look tired, Bill. After you're finished there, you just go right to bed, and I'll bring your dinner up."

"Mae?" Barry asked. "Could you possibly help Bill do this every day? Be sure his leg is cleaned, and then bandaged if the sores are open?"

She bit her lip and shook her head. "I'm not allowed to give my guests any kind of medical services, Mr. Morrow. The county is very firm about that."

Wonderful, Barry thought. It was okay for him or Bill to do it, but Mae, who was probably twice as good at it, was not permitted to touch her guests. "Then could you remind Bill about it every day? Maybe in the morning before he goes to work?"

"Of course."

Barry finished bandaging the leg and stood up. "Okay, Bill. Not let's keep it clean, huh?"

"I'll keep it clean," the old man mumbled. He limped out of the bathroom and shuffled down the hall to his room. Barry watched him, realizing that his irritation had probably come as much from overwork as it had from Bill's transgressions. "Bill?" he called out.

Bill turned and looked back meekly.

"I'll pick you up tomorrow morning. Okay, buddy?"

Bill stared uncertainly at him, then smiled. "Okay, buddy."

Barry followed Mae down the stairs and started for the front door, suddenly feeling exhausted.

"Mr. Morrow," Mae said, "could I talk to you for a minute?"

"I think I'd better get on home, Mae."

"It's rather important," she said. "And it concerns Bill."

118

What now? Barry wondered. "Okay," he said and followed her into the kitchen. Kenny was seated at the table reading a newspaper. He looked up sharply and blushed, then pulled himself awkwardly to his feet.

"How are you, Kenny?" Barry asked.

"Okay. I'd better go to my room," he mumbled and strode quickly through the door.

Mae went for the coffee pot and brought two cups back to the table. "The man from the Housing Authority was here yesterday," she said.

Barry sat down across from her. "Oh? Is everything okay?"

"Well . . . not exactly," she said. "Some of the neighbors have been complaining."

"About what?"

"About all of my guests. About Angela and Bill."

"What do you mean? Why are they complaining?"

"It's been going on for some time now. For years in fact. So it's not just Bill. They don't like the idea of having neighbors who are not . . . normal."

Barry snorted. "And I suppose they're all good upstanding citizens with impeccable breeding? Good normal Americans?"

Mae laughed. "They think so. One in particular. A woman named Mrs. Turner. She's been over here twice since Bill came. She says I'm breaking the law having so many boarders in the house. I think she filed a complaint."

"And what does the Housing Authority have to say?"

"Well, that's the problem. The man came yesterday. A man named Mr. Wynhart. He said the house isn't big enough for three guests. There's only one bathroom upstairs, and I'm supposed to have at least two. He said they're going to revoke my permit to run a boardinghouse."

Barry groaned inwardly; that's all he needed right now.

"I don't understand it," Mae said. "Years ago, I had

119

four guests living here and nobody said a word. Before that, when my mother was alive she sometimes had five or six."

Barry had never thought about Mae Driscoll having a mother. "How long has this place been a rooming house?"

"Oh, gosh, I don't know. I was born in this house sixty-four years ago. And my father and mother had been taking in people for a long time before that." She laughed. "I grew up with people like Angela and Bill as playmates. I think my father took in every stray and unfortunate that came along when I was a little girl. After he died my mother just kept on doing it. And then she died about twelve years ago, and I just kept up the family tradition."

Barry smiled wryly to himself. So he had thought of himself as a minor hero for having saved Bill from Grandville. But Mae and her family had been doing the same thing all their lives. "So why are the neighbors suddenly complaining?" he asked.

"Well, a lot of new people have moved in around here in the last few years. They've been tearing down the old houses and putting up fancy new ones. You probably noticed how the neighborhood is changing. I've had lots of offers to sell the property—from people who want to tear down the house and put up something new. And I guess the new neighbors thought I would sell sooner or later and be gone. But when I took Bill in I guess they realized I was staying."

"Can they revoke your permit after all these years?"

She shrugged. "I guess they can. Things are so complicated these days, with all the laws about zoning and everything. It didn't used to be that way. Back when I was a little girl this house was way out in the country, and we had chickens and pigs and goats, and anything else we wanted. And everybody in town thought it was wonderful the way we helped so many unfortunate people. In fact in all those years there was only one complaint that I remember. That was back in the

Depression, and I think my father was feeding every hobo and unemployed man who came through Iowa. But the town busybody thought he was attracting a 'bad element' to the town, and she complained to the town council. So the council voted a resolution commending Daddy for his charitable work. It was all very funny, really. They gave him a certificate saying he was the humanitarian of the year, and that he should keep up the good work."

Things had certainly changed, Barry reflected. "How did your father make a living?"

"He had a farm implements business. He sold things like tractors and harvesting machines, things like that. But he went broke during the Depression, the same as everybody else. Then he became a traveling salesman for an auto parts company. But he never made much money after that. This house is about all he left. Then, after the war, they build a lot of new houses around here, and that's when they made us get a permit to run a boardinghouse."

It was a sad story, probably duplicated in a hundred small towns across America. "Is this definite?" Barry asked. "What did this guy, Mr. . . ."

"Mr. Wynhart?"

"Yeah. What'd he say? Does he just want Bill to get out?"

"No, I guess it's not that simple. Mr. Wynhart was very nice about it, really. And very sympathetic. But he said my license should have been revoked a long time ago. The house just isn't up to the standards required for roominghouses. It's not just the shortage of bathrooms. It's the old plumbing, insufficient kitchen equipment . . . no ramps for handicapped people . . . all kinds of things. But they've been overlooking it for years and renewing my permit because nobody complained specifically about those things. Then, a couple of weeks ago, I guess one of the neighbors looked it all up in the law books. Mrs. Turner, I suppose. Anyhow, they made a formal complaint, and Mr. Wynhart had to come out and investigate."

"So how long do you have?"

"About two weeks. Maybe a little longer. Mr. Wynhart said he might be able to stall it a week or so by delaying the paperwork."

It sounded bad; not only for Bill, but for Mae and Kenny and Angela too. "What'll you do?"

She shrugged and laughed. "I guess I'll have to sell the place. Let somebody tear it down and put in a nice little suburban number with a swimming pool and sauna. But I won't get much out of it. I'm mortgaged up to my eyeballs."

She had a great attitude toward her bad luck. "Maybe you could get the town council to pass another resolution," Barry said.

She shook her head. "Not today. People are too comfortable and prosperous. Times are a little tough, but they're nothing like the thirties. Back then people were good to each other. And nobody put on airs about being better than anybody else. No, these days the town council is all for progress. And there's no profit in taking care of people like Angela and Kenny and Bill. Nobody even wants to hear about them. They're embarrassing. They'd rather have them go someplace else, or disappear in an institution somewhere." She caught herself and smiled. "I shouldn't say things like that. There are lots of good people in the world. It's just the Mrs. Turners who turn the barrel sour sometimes."

Angela stomped into the room wearing her meanest Shirley Temple face. "I'm hungry, Mae. When are we gonna eat?!"

"Right away, dear," Mae answered. "Keep your pants on."

Barry looked at his watch; it was past six o'clock. He emptied his coffee and rose. "Thanks for the coffee, Mae. And I'll start looking around for a place for Bill."

"Something'll turn up," she said cheerfully.

*   *   *

"How can they do such a thing?" Bev said. "It's terrible! They can't just throw people out on the street." She put Barry's dinner on the table and sat down to finish her own.

"They do it every day," Barry answered. "Angela and Kenny and Bill either find another place, or they go into institutions."

"But it's so ridiculous. How much does it cost the county to take care of people in institutions? About fifty thousand dollars a year?"

"About that. But what other choices do they have? Do you want to take them all in?"

She ignored the question. "Wouldn't it be cheaper and better for everybody concerned, if the county or the state got another place for Mae and paid her to take care of them?"

"Probably," Barry agreed. "But where do you suggest the place be located? Next door to Mrs. Turner?"

It was an impossible circle, and Barry was tired of thinking about it. He had decided to ignore the big problem of trying to correct society's ills and confine his efforts to finding another place for Bill.

XIII

Florence Archer was having a bad day. She had promised the children they could finger-paint in the morning, and neither of her student teachers had shown up at the critical time. Some guest lecturer from the University of Chicago was conducting a seminar and they both had been required to attend. So Florence was left with twenty-five squealing four-year-olds, each of them splattering more paint on the floor than on the paper. And then, as if to aggravate her even more, the strange-looking old man was outside sweeping the playground again.

Until two weeks ago, the cleaning of the playground was handled with quick dispatch by two young men who zipped through the whole operation and had the job done in a couple of hours. But now, the old man Amy Hill called "Bill," was making a life-long career of it. He pushed the leaves here and there with his broom, and dug into cracks and crevices for stems and sticks and tiny bits of nothing. And now, picking them up one by one, he was taking the leaves out of the sandbox, carrying each leaf halfway across the playground to the trash cans, then coming back for another one. At the rate he was working, there was no point in her holding up the children's recess until after he was gone. He wouldn't have the sandbox cleared until dark.

"All right, children," she called out above the din of noise. "Let's all put the lids back on our paint jars, and then put the jars over on the table by the wall."

"But I'm not finished, Miz Archer."

"That's all right, Andrew. We'll finish tomorrow. And everybody take his paintbrush to the wash basin. Wash them all out, and wash your hands, please."

Pre-schoolers were a pleasure to teach; no back talk, and no whining. They always did as they were told, and usually did it in good spirits.

Amy Hill was the last to carry her paint jars to the table. She was a meticulous little girl, and she carefully screwed on each cap and then crossed the room and waited until the others were gone before she put the jars neatly in a row. Then she patiently waited for the others before she washed her hands and paintbrush. She was a fragile little thing, and Florence often wondered about her health. No matter what the temperature, she always arrived at school in a heavy coat and wool mittens.

"All right," Florence said when Amy was finished. "Now let's all go out and have recess, shall we?" She crossed the room and pushed the door open, and they all hurried to go out.

"Amy? May I speak to you for a moment?"

Amy stopped obediently and threw a wistful glance at the man sweeping outside. "Yes, Miss Archer."

Florence took her by the hand and they both sat down on one of the little benches just inside the door. "Amy, I know you think that man out there is your friend."

"He *is* my friend," she said quickly.

"I know, dear, and it is very nice to have friends. But it's not always wise for little girls your age to make friends with old men. It's also good for you to get some exercise during recess time, Amy. That's the purpose of it. After we've sat in a classroom all morning, it's good for us to be physically active for a while. That's why we have the swings and slides and climbing bars in the playground."

Amy dropped her gaze to the floor and bit her lip. "I don't like the swings and slides, Miss Archer."

Florence took one of her hands. Before she could speak, the door opened behind her. It was the maintenance man, today wearing an engineer's cap. "Isn't Amy coming out?" he asked.

"She'll be out in a minute. Please close the door."

"Hi, Amy," the man said.

"Please!" Florence said stiffly to the man.

He backed away and closed the door.

"Can I go, please?" Amy asked. "I want to tell Bill something."

"What is it you want to tell him?"

"I want to tell him my cat had kittens last night."

Florence realized that short of keeping Amy inside, there was no way she could stop her from talking to the man. She would have to handle the situation differently. "All right, Amy," she said with a smile.

On the surface it all seemed harmless enough, she thought as she watched Amy and the old man cross the playground to a bench and sit down. But the man was certainly not normal, and the chance of something untoward happening was just not worth the risk. When they came to pick up their children in the afternoons, several of the parents had already asked about the old man. Florence had casually dismissed their concerns by simply saying he was a staff janitor. But she couldn't let this relationship with Amy continue any longer.

And why, she wondered, had a man like that been hired in the first place? The more she thought about that question, the more it puzzled her. Was he somebody's relative who'd been given a sinecure?

After lunch when the two student teachers finally arrived, Florence left them in charge and strode over to the Maintenance Department. Ed Jenkins was curled over some papers at his desk, puffing his cigar. "Hi, Florence," he said when he saw her at the door. "Come on in. Have a seat."

"No, thank you, Ed. I just have a couple questions."

"Okay, shoot."

"Who is the man you have cleaning up the children's playground?"

Jenkins sat back and took the cigar butt from his mouth. "You mean ol' Bill? He's a nice old guy. Why? Ain't he doin' a good job?"

"I won't bother going into that. What I'm more concerned about is his talking to the children."

"Oh? What's the matter with that?"

Florence didn't feel like going through a thirty minute discourse on why it was not a good idea for four-year-olds to become friendly with old men. "I would just rather not have him talking to them, Ed," she said. "And from what I've seen of him, the man does not appear to be normal."

"There's nothing wrong with him. He's just a little retarded."

"And he's employed by the University?!"

Uh-oh, Jenkins thought. He had forgotten that Florence Archer was Chairwoman of the Faculty Committee, and was always drumming for stiffer hiring requirements for faculty members. She probably felt the same way about anybody else who worked for the University. "Well now, look, Florence. If you really feel that strong about it, I'll see if there's some other place I can put Bill. There's no problem. I can probably stick him somewhere else first thing in the morning."

She wasn't listening. Her chin was up and she was squinting coldly at him. "Who put you up to this, Ed? Is this one of Tom Walz's little projects?"

"Well..."

"Did Tom Walz ask you to hire that man?"

Jenkins pulled himself out of the chair and moved slowly around the desk. "Now, listen, Florence, there's no reason why you should be worried about ol' Bill."

Her squint had turned to a glare. "I think you've answered all of my questions, Mr. Jenkins." She turned and strode out of the room.

Jenkins leaned on the desk and watched through the window as she marched across the grass directly toward the Social Work building. Then he reached for the phone and punched three numbers.

"Tom," he said when he got past the secretary, "this is Ed. In about two minutes I think you're going to have a very hot visitor. Florence Archer is rumbling across the campus with steam coming out her ears. She wants to talk to you about the high professional standards of the University staff, and a certain person named Bill Sackter...Right. Good luck."

It had to happen sooner or later. But Tom Walz hadn't expected it to come from Florence Archer. He had a few enemies within his own department who would have been delighted to use Bill Sackter as a bargaining weapon. But Florence Archer would be tougher to deal with. She was motivated by lofty principles rather than political ambitions.

Walz cleared some of the debris from his desk and told his secretary to usher Florence in as quickly as she arrived. He didn't have long to wait. He was still carrying stacks of folders to the file cabinet when the door swung open and she marched in, ready for battle.

"Florence, how good to see you." He left the fold-

127

ers on the cabinet and came smiling back to his desk. "Can I have Susan get you a cup of coffee?"

"No," she said and got straight to business. "You can tell me why you told Ed Jenkins to hire that old man who wears the silly hats."

"Please sit down, Florence. I'm sure you've been on your feet all day."

She sat down, but she didn't look comfortable. She lifted her chin and glared at him, waiting.

"I suppose you're talking about Bill Sackter," Walz said as casually as he could.

"Indeed I am."

"I see." He eased back in his chair and frowned. "It's an interesting situation with Bill Sackter. He's from Minneapolis, you know."

"I don't care where he's from. I just don't think my children should be part of one of your experiments to reform society."

"What are you talking about?"

"I'm talking about Bill Sackter."

"And what does Bill Sackter have to do with my so-called experiments to reform society?"

"I am not an ogre, Tom, and I am not against the idea of helping disabled people. But that man is working around a class of pre-school children. He wanders in and out of my classroom, and I'm getting all kinds of pressure from parents who come by the school. I can't predict how he may behave with the children at any point, and I don't believe you can either."

Walz was silent a moment, hoping the pause would slow her down. "I've checked Bill out very carefully, Florence. Barry Morrow has known him for years. And, after all, this is a school of social work. We have an obligation to foster a humane attitude toward the handicapped."

"And I have an obligation to insure the safety of my children."

"Of course you do, but Bill isn't dangerous."

"Would you like to make a big poster informing

the parents of that fact and hang it in the school grounds? And can you really guarantee the man is not dangerous? The man is retarded, Tom. Nobody can predict what he might do from one minute to the next. And why should a man like that be allowed to come in contact with young children? We simply can't take the risk of something happening."

She had a point. But the problem could be easily resolved. "This really isn't that serious, Florence. I'm sure Ed Jenkins can find some other spot for Bill; someplace far away from your school. I agree, it was probably a mistake to put him over there." He sat forward and smiled, but Florence was still simmering.

"You can move him somewhere else, Tom, but that is not the real issue here."

"Oh? And what is the real issue?"

"It involves the hiring standards of the entire University. They should be no different for the maintenance workers than they are for the faculty or the administration. You just can't do this sort of thing. It's unfair to the other people who work here, and it's unfair to people who would *like* to work for the University. You do it in the Maintenance Department, and next is the Security Department, and everywhere else. I won't let you do it, Tom."

"Oh, come on, Florence. It's not really *that* serious."

"I'm serious about it. And if you insist on keeping him, I'm calling a meeting of the faculty advisors next week to discuss the problem."

Walz sat back and smiled grimly to himself. Florence Archer should be carrying a cross and leading the French armies against the British. But he knew her threat was real, and that she would have no trouble persuading the other faculty advisors that she was right.

"Okay, Florence. Maybe you're right. Could you give me a couple of days to straighten it out? In the meantime I'll tell Ed Jenkins to keep Bill away from the school."

She appeared to be surprised by the easy victory. She almost smiled as she pulled herself to her feet. "Very well. I'll wait until next week. But if something isn't done by then, I'm going ahead with this, Tom. In the meantime I don't expect to see that man around again."

"You won't, Florence. And thanks for bringing it to my attention."

After the door closed, Walz rose and moved to the window where he watched the crowds of students going to and from classes. Sometimes he wished he'd become a plumber instead of a teacher.

So what to do with Bill? Bill Sackter was really not his responsibility. Nor was the welfare of a thousand others like him. But a man either practiced what he preached, or he found himself a new profession. So he'd better call Ed Jenkins and Barry Morrow. And then do some hard thinking about how to circumvent the University employment rules again.

"You mean it's not good enough just to give Bill a job somewhere else on the campus?" Barry asked.

Tom Walz had been waiting outside the door when Barry's two o'clock class ended, and they walked toward the cafeteria to get a cup of coffee.

"It's not good enough for Florence," he said and chuckled. "She's appointed herself the conscience of the University, and all the rules must be obeyed. In her mind, if Bill continues to work here, the entire institution will collapse in a matter of days."

"What're we going to do?"

"We're going to think very hard and come up with some other kind of scam, I guess. I don't suppose Bill can drive a car?"

"No."

"To bad. The president of the University is looking for a chauffeur. Or maybe we could make Bill president. It's a good job for someone who likes to eat chicken and deliver meaningless speeches to prospective donors."

Barry laughed, picturing Bill with a pile of chicken in front of him. And Bill was certainly capable of delivering meaningless speeches. "Well, the whole problem may be academic anyway," he said. "It looks like Mae Driscoll and all of her tenants are going to be evicted, and I haven't had any luck finding another place for Bill."

"Why is she being evicted?"

"Her house doesn't meet the requirements for a boardinghouse, and the neighbors have complained. Apparently they're cancelling her license."

Walz suddenly stopped and watched two men carry a file cabinet out of a sub-basement. "What are you doing?" he asked.

"Clearing out that room," one of the men said as they hoisted the cabinet onto a truck. "The fire department says it's a firetrap and we have to clear it out."

Walz went down the four steps and peered into the room. Barry followed him. It was a gloomy area about twenty by twenty and filled with old file cabinets, stacks of cardboard boxes and loose papers.

"What is all this stuff?" Walz asked as the two men squeezed past them.

"Old records from the Registrar's Office. It's all been put on microfilm now."

"What are you gonna do with it?"

"Take it over to the dump and burn it."

"Huh," Walz grunted. He took a final look at the room and they resumed walking. "You mean they're throwing Mae Driscoll out just because of Bill?"

"No. Apparently she's been in violation of the codes for years. But nobody complained until Bill showed up."

"Maybe you ought to go down to City Hall and talk to them. It's possible Mae misunderstood something."

"I've already got an appointment," Barry said. "Ten o'clock Saturday morning."

*   *   *

Bill liked his new job. It was in the Physical Education Department on the far side of the campus, and he swept out the halls of the building, and then swept the gym and the locker rooms.

"It's just temporary," Ed Jenkins told him as he drove him over on the first morning. "The guy who usually does it had to go to Philadelphia for a while because his mother's sick. So you'll do the sweeping till he gets back. Then Mr. Walz'll find something else for you."

"Why can't I sweep at the playground anymore?" Bill asked. "I liked doing that. I liked the children. Especially Amy."

"Yeah ... well, I guess they don't want that swept anymore."

It was very busy in the Physical Education building. Bill started at the top and worked his way down to the first floor and got every speck of dust and dirt swept up. He smiled at the students passing by, and they were all friendly and smiled back. Then he watched a group of young men swimming in a big pool, wondering what it was like to jump in the water the way they did. He'd never been in any water deeper than a bathtub, and it looked like fun. He leaned on his broom, twisted his neck and watched some of the boys climb a ladder and dive head-first into the water from platforms almost as high as the ceiling. Then everybody jumped out of the pool and disappeared, and he realized he was hungry and it was lunchtime.

He retrieved his lunchpail from where he'd left it in the broom closet and headed across the campus, eating his sandwich on the way. He couldn't wait to tell Amy about his new job, and how friendly everybody was, and how the boys jumped into the pool like they were birds diving into a lake.

When he came within sight of the playground, the children were already filing back into the classroom. He hurried, looking hard for Amy in the group, hoping she would wait outside for him. But the children all disappeared and the door closed before he got there.

He sat on the bench where he usually sat and talked with Amy, and he finished his lunch watching the windows of the classroom. Maybe she would see him, and she would come out for a minute.

Yesterday she'd said she would give him one of her kittens, and Bill had asked Mae about it. Mae said it was okay. So he wanted to ask her about the kitten and tell her about the swimmers. He wondered if Amy had ever been in a swimming pool like that one.

He closed his lunchpail and waited some more. But Amy didn't come out. He didn't know what to do.

He looked at the swings and the slides and over at the climbing bars for a while, then he picked up his lunchpail and walked over to the windows of the classroom. It was hard to see through the glass because of the reflections. He put his lunchpail down, cupped his hands around his eyes and peered in.

All of the children were crowded around tables on the far side, and he couldn't see Amy among them. Then a little boy pointed at the windows and laughed, and all the children turned around and looked at him. Miss Archer, the tall skinny teacher, also looked. She put down her paintbrushes she was holding and came striding across the room. She pushed the door open and came out.

"What are you doing here?" she asked.

It sounded like she was mad. Bill picked up his lunchpail and stood with his head down. "I just wanted to talk to Amy."

"You're not supposed to be here. You're not supposed to come around here ever again, Mr. Sackter. Do you understand?"

Bill didn't understand. "I just wanted to talk to Amy," he repeated, almost inaudibly. "I wanted to tell Amy about the swimming pool."

"Well, you can't talk to Amy, and you must leave immediately."

"Why can't I talk to Amy?" he asked.

133

She sighed and pushed the door shut behind her. "I've told you twice now, and this is the last time, Mr. Sackter. You are to leave here immediately, and you are never to come back. Now go, or I will call the campus security guards!"

Bill stared at her wondering why she was so mad at him, and why she didn't want him to ever come back. He must have done something very bad. He couldn't remember anything, but it must have been very bad to make her so angry. "I'm sorry," he said and turned away.

He walked past the sandbox and the swings and up to the walk. "I'm sorry," he mumbled again without looking back.

Saturday morning turned out to be cold and drizzly; a gloomy day that perfectly matched Barry's mood. In the last three days he had spent all of his free time calling boardinghouses, resident hotels, foster homes— any place that might conceivably give Bill a place to live. He had even called three or four fraternity houses, and he had asked all of his students if they knew of any place.

It was amazing how sympathetic everybody was. But it was also amazing how many places were filled up, or had impossible restrictions, or were certain that because Bill was retarded he also must be psychotic and dangerous. The most infuriating response had come from a prim and proper voice of a rooming house owner on the other side of town. "I'd like to help you, Mr. Morrow, but I just couldn't consider having any kind of deviate living among my guests. They're all rather cultured people here, you see, and I'm afraid your friend just wouldn't fit in."

Barry pushed through the doors of the Housing Authority Offices at five minutes to ten, soaking wet and in no mood to hear any more comments about how dangerous or disruptive or upsetting Bill Sackter might be.

The place was quiet and almost empty. The receptionist indifferently instructed him to take the elevator to the fourth floor and follow the corridor to the back of the building. Jack Wynhart's office was the last door on the left.

The office door was open, and Jack Wynhart was talking on the phone when Barry walked in. The man gave him a perfunctory smile and nodded toward a chair. Barry sat down.

The office looked like all government offices Barry had seen: a steel desk, a row of gray filing cabinets, in-out baskets and thick manila folders on every surface that was flat. Wynhart looked to be in his mid-thirties, a nondescript man wearing a white dress shirt and a drab necktie that looked as shopworn as the manila folders on his desk. He was listening more than talking on the phone. "All right, Mr. Gibbel," he finally said without enthusiasm, "I'll certainly look into it. Thank you for calling."

He dropped the phone in its cradle, smiled wearily and reached across to shake Barry's hand. "You're Mr. Morrow, I presume?"

After the handshake, Wynhart settled back into his chair. "Not very nice weather we're having, is it?" he said.

"No," Barry answered and got to the point. "Mae Driscoll tells me, Mr. Wynhart, that you are about to serve an eviction notice on her. Is that right?"

The man laughed and tilted back in his chair, turning a pencil through his fingers. "No, I'm not about to serve an eviction notice on her. Mae Driscoll can live in her house as long as she wants."

"Then what's the problem?" Barry asked.

Wynhart shook his head. "As a private residence, I have no complaints whatsoever concerning the property. But if she wants to run a boardinghouse, certain requirements must be met. Most of them concern the health and safety conditions. That house is more than a hundred years old, Mr. Morrow. And to my knowledge

135

there have never been any improvements in the plumbing or wiring. And building codes have changed considerably in the last hundred years. Secondly, there is the matter of zoning. That area is zoned strictly for single family residences."

"Except that she was there first, long before there were any other residences around. And long before there were any zoning laws."

Wynhart nodded. "Yes...that's true. And that's why we've allowed her to continue operating. But the law is very specific about health and safety requirements in boardinghouses. Particularly when the guests are wards of the state."

"She's always had people who were wards of the government. So why are you suddenly cracking down on her?"

Wynhart lowered his chin and rubbed his forehead. "There's something I want you to understand, Mr. Morrow," he finally said. "I'm on Mae's side. The last thing I want to do is revoke her permit to run a boardinghouse. But I'm in the same position as a policeman. If somebody jaywalks every day on an empty street, and I think the infraction is completely harmless, as a policeman I'll simply overlook it. But if some citizen files a complaint, I simply have no choice but to issue the jaywalker a citation. That's precisely the situation with Mae Driscoll. I think she's an incredible woman, and I think what's she's doing is wonderful. I think it's particularly admirable because there are so few people in the world who will make an effort to help the kind of people she does. If it were up to me, I would let Mae Driscoll take in a dozen boarders." He smiled wearily and reached for a yellow pad on the counter behind him.

"This is a list of every boardinghouse within our jurisdiction. In the past week, I've called every one of them trying to find a place for Angela, Kenny and Bill. I've come up with nothing."

Barry didn't know what to say. He'd come into the

office prepared to pound on the desk and accuse Jack Wynhart of being a combination of Simon Legree and Attila the Hun. Instead he'd found a kindred soul. "So what's going to happen to them?" he asked.

Wynhart shook his head. "What would happen to Bill if he went back to Minnesota?"

He would wither up and die, Barry reflected. "They might find him a place somewhere. But for him it would be going backwards. He would probably become depressed...eventually end up in an institution again. And that would kill him. As far as he's concerned, he's a free man now. What he calls a 'regular good man.'"

Wynhart nodded and tossed his yellow pad back on the counter. "Have you looked into any of the nursing homes around here?" he asked.

"No. I've considered that as sort of a last resort. I'm not so sure that would be a good place for Bill."

"Yes, you may be right. But the 'last resort' may be better than nothing. The best one around here is probably Elm Ridge on the west side of town. You might drive Bill out there and let him take a look. It's run by a woman named Shirley Crandall."

Barry didn't want to think about it. He wasn't even sure that Bill knew he was in danger of being evicted from Mae's house. "Who filed the complaint against Mae?" he asked. "Was it a woman named Mrs. Turner?"

Wynhart pondered the question, turning the pencil in his fingers again. "It really doesn't make any difference," he said circumspectly. "Every citizen has the right—even the duty, I suppose—to report violations of the law. And once the report is filed, I have an obligation to follow through on it."

In spite of Wynhart's sympathies, the situation appeared hopeless. "How long before the permit is revoked?" Barry asked.

"By law, I have to issue notice next Monday. Then she will have ten days."

Barry sighed. "If you will excuse my saying so, in this case I think the law is an ass."

Wynhart smiled. "In this case, I agree with you."

Barry pulled himself out of the chair. "Is there any chance of changing the law? Or getting the city council to vote an exception? Mae tells me they did it fifty years ago."

"Yes, she told me about that. But I'm afraid that politicians today are more responsive to their affluent constituents. Back in the thirties there was no such thing as an affluent constituent. Such a proposal would take about ten seconds to find its way into a commmittee wastebasket."

"Well, thanks for your time, Mr. Wynhart. I came ready for battle, but I can't seem to find any enemies."

Wynhart rose and shook his hand. "That's often the way it is in these situations. Everybody is all in favor of helping out the unfortunates among us. But they always want somebody else to do it. Keep in touch. If there's anything else I can do, let me know."

Barry went back out in the rain feeling like the world was about to come to an end. If the worst happened, he could probably move Bill into his own home. But sooner or later he would need a bigger place, and that was way past his budget now.

XIV

Bill woke up at eight o'clock Saturday morning, but he didn't get out of bed. He switched on his television, and with his eyes half closed he watched *Bugs Bunny* and *Road Runner,* and thought about Amy.

If Miz Archer wouldn't let him go to the playground anymore, he probably would never see Amy again. And Amy had a kitten for him, and she was probably waiting for him to come and get it. So Amy might think he was mad at her or something, and she might give the kitten to somebody else.

It was a terrible problem that he couldn't deal with,

and he stared dully at the television screen, feeling more miserable all the time. He wished he knew where Amy lived, and he wished he knew how to write, so he could write a postcard to her about the swimming pool and how he wanted the kitten.

When the next commercials came on, Bill got out of bed and shuffled to the bathroom where he washed his leg the way Barry had told him to. Then he dressed himself and went down the stairs.

Angela was sitting at the kitchen table with her doll, and Kenny was washing the windows. "You're too late for breakfast," Angela sneered, "and Mae's gone out to do the shopping. And there isn't any coffee left because Kenny drank it all up."

Angela was wearing a white dress with big red polka dots, and her skirt was all starched and sticking out like a little girl going to a party.

"I didn't drink all the coffee," Kenny said. "Angela poured it out in the sink."

"Liar," Angela muttered. She stuck her tongue out at Kenny and turned back to Bill. "So you can't have any coffee because you don't know how to make it, do you."

Mae always had coffee waiting when Bill came down for breakfast. It made him feel good and awake and warm in the morning, and he wanted some very much today. "I know how to make coffee," he said. He picked up the coffee pot from the table and carried it to the sink, trying to remember how Mae did it. He knew she put water in the pot, and put the lid back on. But he couldn't remember what she did after that.

Kenny was watching him from the window. "You gotta put the coffee grounds in that little basket thing," he said.

"Don't tell him!" Angela said sharply. "He said he knows how to do it, so let him do it by himself."

Bill found the coffee can and opened it. A little yellow plastic cup was lying in the grounds.

"Four of those scoops," Kenny said. "All you have

139

to do is put the coffee grounds in the basket. Then you just put the lid back on and put it on the stove."

Bill followed the instructions and put the pot on the stove. He turned the knob and the flame came on.

"I'll bet it'll be terrible coffee," Angela sneered. "I bet you won't be able to drink it."

"It'll be good coffee," Bill answered. He kept his back to Angela and watched the pot, waiting for something to happen.

"It's all your fault, you know," Angela said, "that we have to move out of here."

Bill turned and looked at her. "We don't have to move out of here."

"Yes, we do. We have to move out. All three of us—you and me and Kenny."

Bill turned back to his coffee pot, suddenly finding it hard to breathe. "We don't have to move out. This is where I live now, and my buddy, Barry, said I could live here."

"That's not so," Angela said. "We have to move out of here because Mr. Wynhart is making us move. Isn't that so, Kenny?"

Bill looked quickly at Kenny, who was rubbing hard on the windows. "That's true," Kenny said.

"And it's all because of you," Angela went on. "It's because you're dumb and you don't know how to read or write or do anything. That's what Mae told me last night."

Kenny threw her a dark glance. "She didn't say that."

"Yes, she did. And she said she's going to send me to live in a big house that has lots of servants and a beautiful garden with fountains and statues and grass as far as you can see. And Bill's going to go to an institution. He's going to a bad place where they beat you and they don't give you anything to eat."

Bill kept his eyes on the stove because he was too choked up to say anything. He knew Angela was lying. But Kenny didn't tell lies, and he said they had to move.

"She didn't say any of that stuff," Kenny said. "She just said we have to move."

The coffee pot was making noises and light brown liquid jumped up and splattered inside the glass top. "If we have to move, I'll find a nice place to live," Bill said. "My buddy, Barry'll find a nice place. He'll find a nice place for all of us to live."

"No, he won't," Angela snickered. "Mae said he couldn't find any place. She talked to your buddy last night, and he hasn't found any place at all. You're going to have to go back to an institution with all the crazy people."

"You'd better stop making up things," Kenny said.

"I'm not making up things. She told me last night, and you weren't even there, Kenny. So, ha ha ha."

Bill pulled his shoulders together and concentrated on the coffee pot, not wanting to hear any more from Angela. He wished he had stayed in bed and watched some more *Bugs Bunny* and *Road Runner.*

"When the coffee is dark like that, it means it's all done," Kenny said. "You want me to cook you some eggs?"

"No. Thank you very much." Bill poured coffee into a cup and took it into the living room. Kenny followed him, bringing along his rags and his squirter. "Don't pay any attention to Angela," he said. "Mae's looking for a place to live for us, and so is your buddy. Everything will turn out fine."

"I wanta live here," Bill said.

"Well, I guess Mr. Wynhart isn't going to let us, because it's such an old house. But everything is gonna turn out fine. That's what Mae said." He smiled at Bill and squirted cleaner on the front window.

Bill sipped his coffee and wondered why Barry hadn't said anything to him about moving. Then he remembered that Barry was mad at him for getting lost and going downtown and being pinched. He was also mad at him because he hadn't taken care of his leg. Maybe that was why he hadn't said anything. And maybe that was why Miz Archer was mad at him and wouldn't let him talk to Amy anymore.

Bill felt tired and a little sick to his stomach. Everybody was mad at him, and some man named Mr. Wynhart was going to make them move out of the house, probably just because of him. When his coffee was all gone, he sat for a long time staring at the carpet, wishing he had never come to Iowa, and that he was back in Minnesota living at the country club.

"What's the matter, Bill?" Kenny asked when he finished with the windows.

"I wanta talk to my sister Sarah," Bill said.

"Don't she live in Florida?"

"Uh-huh. An' I want to talk to her."

"You got her phone number?"

Bill pulled out his wallet. "Yeah, I got it right here. Miz Keating gave it to me. Would you call her on the telephone for me?"

Kenny scratched his head and sat on the arm of the sofa. "Well, I don't know as Mae would like that, Bill. I mean Florida's a long way off."

"I'd sure like to talk to Sarah, Kenny. I've never talked to her before, an' she's the only sister I got. Miz Keating said she's livin' in a nurses' home, so I guess she's a nurse."

Kenny rubbed his nose and frowned at the carpet for a minute, thinking. Then he got up. "Well, okay, I'll dial it for ya."

Bill quickly rose and followed him. "Thank you very much, Kenny. You're my buddy."

The telephone was at a little table next to the stairs. Kenny put the piece of paper on the table and carefully dialed the number. He listened for a minute, then handed the phone to Bill.

"Sarah?" he said.

"This is the Bayview Nursing Home," a woman's voice said. "May I help you, sir?"

"I want to talk to my sister. Her name is Sarah, and she lives there."

"Can you tell me her last name, sir?"

"Her last name is Sarah Sackter because she's my sister."

The woman was silent for a minute. "The only Sarah we have here is Sarah Millard. Would that be her?"

"Sarah Millard?" Bill had never heard of a Sarah Millard.

Kenny touched his arm and pointed at the piece of paper with the telephone number on it. "That's it," he said. "Sarah Millard."

"Oh. Yes, that's her, Sarah Millard," Bill said into the phone.

There were some clicks on the phone and a shaky voice answered.

"Is that you, Sarah? This is Bill. Your brother Bill. Remember?"

Sarah didn't say anything for a long time. "My brother Billy?" she asked. Her voice was very weak and shaky.

"That's right." Bill grinned at Kenny. 'She calls me Billy." He turned back to the phone. "How you doin', Sarah?"

"Oh, I been real sick, Billy. I been in this place for a long time. How are you?"

Bill grinned, feeling warm and good for the first time today. "Oh, I'm just fine, Sarah. I got me a job, an' I been workin' an' savin' my money, an' I'm gonna come to Florida and see you real soon 'cause I can't live here any more. How would you like that, if I came to see you? I can ride a bus now without anybody needing to help me or anything."

"I've been real sick, Billy."

She sounded like she was out of breath. "I know you been sick, Sarah. Miz Keating told me that, an' that's why I wanna come and see you."

"Oh, Billy..." She was crying and couldn't talk.

"Don't feel bad, Sarah. Don't cry. You just lie down and rest an' you wait for me. I'm comin' to Florida an' I'll take care of you, Sarah."

"Hello?" a strange voice said. "Who is this?"

143

"This is Bill. This is Sarah's brother, Bill. What happened to Sarah?"

"I'm sorry, but Mrs. Millard is very tired. Could you call back some other time when she's feeling better?"

"Oh. Well . . . sure. You tell Sarah to take it easy, an' I'll call her again before I come. You tell her I been savin' up and I'll see her real soon."

"I'll tell her. Goodbye."

"Goodbye," Bill said. He held the phone at his ear for a minute, hoping Sarah might come back on. But she didn't. He put it back in the cradle.

"What happened?" Kenny asked.

"Oh, she's just fine. She was real happy to talk to me, but she was tired. She had to lay down."

"Oh," Kenny said.

Bill smiled and nodded and tucked the telephone number back in his wallet. He rose and slowly climbed the stairs, feeling a little tired. "I think I'll go lay down for a while," he sighed.

"The reason I didn't tell you," Barry said, "was that I didn't want you to get upset. I was hoping to find some new place for you first, and then you wouldn't be worrying about it all that time."

Bill nodded and looked out the side window of the car. They had driven all the way through town, and now they were passing by farmhouses and plowed fields. It was a cold day and it felt like it was going to start snowing at any minute. "Mae got the letter from Mr. Wynhart on Thursday," Bill said.

"I know she did. Listen, Bill. I don't know what this place is like, but Mr. Wynhart said it was very nice. It's called a nursing home, but it doesn't mean you have to be sick to live there."

Bill thought about Sarah and how tired she sounded. "I'd rather live some place with Mae and Kenny and Angela. I don't like nursing homes."

"I thought you didn't like Angela."

It was true, he didn't like Angela. But he felt like

the four of them were a family and it wouldn't be quite right without Angela. "Sarah lives in a nursing home and she's very sick. I talked to her on the telephone. I told her I might go and visit her. I been saving my money."

Barry smiled at him, and drove on in silence.

Bill had flatly refused to go look at the nursing home when Barry first proposed it. He said he was going to stay in Mae's house no matter what happened, because Mae needed him. He had learned how to make coffee now, and for the past week he had been making coffee every morning. He had also scrubbed the floors and vacuumed the carpets, and he was helping Mae wash the dishes every night.

It sounded like Bill was working hard at all the household chores hoping that his industriousness would somehow magically reinstate Mae's boardinghouse license. Barry had finally explained to him that there was no way any of them could stay in the house, and that the sooner they started looking at other places the better off he was going to be. So Bill had finally gotten his coat and trudged out to the car to go look at the Elm Ridge Nursing Home. But whether the place looked like a pigsty or a palatial mansion, Barry had his doubts about Bill liking it. Like everybody else in the world, Bill wanted to be around friends and family.

Tom Walz still hadn't come up with a permanent solution for Bill's employment problem. And apparently Florence Archer had come storming into his office again because Bill had been hanging around her children's playground. Barry hadn't heard about it until the end of the week, and he still hadn't decided how to broach the question to Bill. He was a little apprehensive about what kind of answer he might get.

"How do you like your new job?" he asked.

Bill nodded, still staring out at the scenery. "I like it fine."

"You like it better than working at the playground?"

"No," Bill said. "I liked it better over there."

"Why?"

"I liked to watch the children. And I liked to talk to Amy."

Barry gave him a quick glance. "Who's Amy?"

"She's my friend. She was going to give me a kitten. Mae said I could have it in the house, and Amy was going to give it to me."

"So what happened?"

Bill frowned and rubbed his nose and looked out the window again. "They didn't want me to sweep the playground anymore, and I couldn't talk to Amy."

"Have you gone back there since you got the new job?"

"Uh-huh. But I couldn't talk to Amy. Miz Archer told me to go away." Bill's voice suddenly thickened, as if he were going to cry. "She told me not to ever come back there anymore."

Barry sighed, feeling a measure of relief. He had never seen anything in Bill's behavior to suggest he had anything but a wholesome attitude toward children. Florence Archer's vociferous complaints to Tom Walz, however, had prompted Barry to wonder if there might be some basis for her fears. But the supposedly dangerous old man simply wanted a kitten. And for that, Florence Archer was threatening to have a faculty meeting and tear the roof off the University if Bill wasn't banished to Siberia. Barry decided he would have a little chat with Florence Archer if she insisted on that meeting.

"Maybe we can work something out so you can talk to Amy again," he said.

Bill looked at him and brightened. "Okay," he said and nodded.

The Elm Ridge Nursing Home was in a pretty setting of elms and birches, with a white picket fence surrounding an acre of well-landscaped grounds. The main building was a low, rambling structure connected to several others by covered walks. Barry came to a stop in the parking lot and Bill gave the place a long, brooding look.

"I don't like this place," he said.

"You haven't seen it yet," Barry answered. "And that's the same thing you said about Mae's house when you first saw it. Come on, let's take a look."

Bill slowly got out of the car and followed Barry up the walk to the front door. Barry opened it for him and then had to nudge him through with a hand on his elbow.

The lobby looked like a doctor's office: all clean and sterile, with potted plants, plastic couches and all the popular magazines neatly arranged on low coffee tables. A red-haired receptionist with thick glasses was erasing something from the paper in her typewriter. "May I help you?" she asked without looking up.

"We have an appointment with Mrs. Crandall," Barry said.

She reached over, pressed three buttons on her phone and announced their presence, then resumed her erasing. "She'll be out in a minute."

Barry sat down on a couch and Bill sat at the far end. "Nice and quiet here," Bill said with a touch of sarcasm.

"Well, that's just out here. They have activity rooms, you know. Games and singing . . . all that sort of thing."

Bill nodded faintly, then reached in his pocket and pulled out his harmonica. He played three or four notes before the receptionist gave him a sharp look. "Shhhhh!" she hissed.

Bill returned the harmonica to his pocket and glanced at Barry. "Yup. Sure is nice and quiet here."

Mrs. Crandall came striding through the door a moment later, smiling happily, her rubber-soled shoes squeaking on the linoleum. She was a tall, slender woman with short, neatly brushed gray hair, and a pale green dress that looked almost like a uniform. "Hi, there!" she bubbled, and extended a hand as she strode over to Bill. "You must be Bill. Welcome to Elm Ridge Nursing Home."

Bill gave her a limp hand and said nothing.

Barry quickly rose. "I'm Barry Morrow. We talked on the phone." He drew Mrs. Crandall toward the receptionist's desk as he spoke. "Try not to mention 'nursing home,'" he said softly. "Bill doesn't like the sound of it."

"Of course," she said enthusiastically, and turned back to the couch. "So, Bill...what would you like to see first?"

Bill pulled himself reluctantly to his feet. "Where they keep the people," he muttered.

Mrs. Crandall chuckled and led them into a corridor. "We don't exactly 'keep' people here, Bill. Our residents have complete freedom of the grounds."

The corridor was lined with paintings, all of them with price tags dangling from their frames. Mrs. Crandall made a broad gesture toward them as they moved along. "These acrylics, by the way, were all done by our residents, and they're reasonably priced. I think they make delightful gifts."

"Finterpaints," Bill muttered.

"Well, yes, some of them do resemble fingerpaints, don't they. You're very perceptive, Bill."

Bill wasn't impressed by the compliment. His face darkened as he glanced through the opened doors they passed.

What he saw could not be very encouraging, and even Barry clenched his teeth. In one room a wrinkled old woman was stretched out on a bed, moaning softly, her head rocking from side to side. In another, a nurse was struggling with a half-naked man, trying to make him lie down. In other rooms people were staring vacantly at the floor, or talking to themselves, or simply sleeping. Barry was reminded of Grandville.

They had to detour around a straggle-haired woman who was rocking her doll in the middle of the corridor. Bill stopped and frowned at her. "You know a lady named Angela?" he asked.

Mrs. Crandall quickly came back and escorted the woman into a room. "Now, you stay out of the hall, Edna." She shut the door firmly and came smiling back to resume the tour.

"Now, this is what we call our efficiency room," she said a moment later and gestured through an open door. "Would you like to take a look, Bill?"

Bill stepped inside and Barry followed. The room consisted of four white walls and a single window. In the corner a door opened into a bathroom the size of a broom closet.

"It has it's own bathroom, of course," Mrs. Crandall said, "and a good deal of closet space, as you can see."

The closet was a painted steel cabinet about four feet wide. Barry forced himself to smile at Bill. "A little furniture could make it homey."

"I just got a TV," Bill muttered.

"And we have furnished rooms, also," Mrs. Crandall said. "They're very reasonable."

Bill walked over and stared at the blank wall. "Mostly I got caps," he said. "All over my wall."

"That would be fine," Mrs. Crandall said. She smiled at Barry. "It's important that they make the room their own."

Bill was still looking at the wall, as if trying to judge the dimensions of it. "I got about a million caps," he said. "I pound nails and hang 'em up." He nodded to himself. "Yup, I pound 'em all the time. One million caps...one million nails. An' I like to move 'em around so they don't always look the same. I pound and pound the nails, and then I pull 'em out and pound 'em in again in different places. I like to do that...pound and pound and pound."

Barry stared at Bill, amazed. He'd never heard Bill say such a thing, and he knew it wasn't true. Mrs. Crandall was also staring, but looked frightened as if she believed every word of it. Her happy smile had frozen solid, and she blinked uncertainly from Bill to Barry.

Barry smiled back at her. "Uh...perhaps Bill would like to think it over for a day or two, Mrs. Crandall."

"Would you like to see the recreation rooms?" Mrs. Crandall asked. Her voice was no longer bubbly and she was wringing her hands. Bill gazed indifferently at her, as if totally unaware of the reaction he had caused.

"I don't think that will be necessary," Barry said. "I'm sure they're very nice, but I think we'd better be going."

The woman followed them to the door, thanking them for coming. "I have some other people looking at the rooms today," she said as Barry and Bill went out. "So it's quite possible I won't have anything available if you come back."

"I understand, Mrs. Crandall," Barry said. "And thanks for everything."

Bill walked out to the parking lot, his gait noticeably bouncier than when they arrived.

Barry said nothing until they were headed back toward town. Then he gave Bill a hard look. "You did that deliberately, didn't you, Bill."

"Did what?" Bill asked.

Barry couldn't blame him. The Elm Ridge Nursing Home looked like a way station on the road to a cemetery. He sighed and shrugged. "Never mind."

So what now? he wondered. His "last resort" had turned out to be a hellhole, and he didn't have any more ideas.

"I think I'll just stay with Mae and Kenny and Angela," Bill said casually.

Barry glanced at him and started to explain the situation, but then thought better of it. There was nothing Bill could do about the dilemma. So there was no point in upsetting him any more than necessary.

"What's so infuriating," Barry said to Bev after he got home, "is that Mae's is such a perfect place for him.

He thinks Mae and Kenny are wonderful, and in some strange way I think he likes Angela too. And because of some narrow-minded neighbors and some old plumbing, all four of them are going to have their lives shattered."

He sat cross-legged on the floor, with Clay hanging onto his fingers and trying to stand up. "Blugh," Clay said and tumbled forward.

Bev brought Clay's bowl of baby food over to the coffee table. "It seems hard to believe that there's nobody in this whole city who will take him in."

"It's more complicated than that," Barry replied. "They probably would have taken him at the nursing home if Bill hadn't sabotaged the whole thing." Barry smiled and hoisted Clay into Bev's lap. "I really didn't realize he was that clever—or subtle. But he scared Mrs. Crandall to death with his little act."

"Aren't there some county homes that might take him? They must have other people like Bill in Iowa."

"Except they're all filled up, and the local people get preference. And I'm not sure Bill could survive in a place like that anyway."

Bev nodded, and Barry knew she was thinking the same thing he was. "We could take him in here," she said tentatively. "At least temporarily . . . until you found something else for him."

Barry wondered if it was really feasible. Just as they had warned him when he brought Bill to Iowa, he made a lot of demands on people; simply because in a lot of ways he was helpless. There was also the question of space. Barry had moved all his film and projection equipment into the spare room, and was now using it for an office. Sooner or later the room would be Clay's, but it was going to be crowded.

"Yes, it's a thought," he said. "But we've still got a little time."

XV

Barry might have seen the notice on the bulletin board, but he had been busy all week. Even then he might have missed it, but he had gone into the faculty lounge looking for Dr. Brennan, one of the creative writing professors, when he spotted the sheet of pale green paper.

FACULTY ADVISORS MEETING
At the request of Florence Archer, an extraordinary meeting of the Faculty Advisors will be held this Friday afternoon at three o'clock in the Social Science conference room. The subject for consideration will be University hiring and employment practices. All members of the committee are urged to attend.

There was no doubt in Barry's mind about what the real subject of the meeting would be: the employment in the Maintenance Department of a retarded man named Bill Sackter. And the meeting was scheduled to start in twenty minutes.

It was a quarter of a mile walk over to the Social Science building, and Barry's blood pressure rose a notch every step of the way. He was not a member of the Advisory Committee, and therefore had no voice in their proceedings or deliberations. But he was having enough trouble helping Bill survive without contending with the petty prejudices of people like Florence Archer.

She was the only person in the conference room, and she was seated at the end of the long oak table sorting papers when Barry came through the door. She glared at him as if he had climbed through the window of her bedroom. "May I help you?" she asked stiffly.

152

He stopped at the other end of the table and gripped the back of a chair. "You can help me very much, Miss Archer," he said. "I don't think we've formally met, but my name is Barry Morrow. I'm a friend of Bill Stackter."

Her face hardened and she took some more papers out of a briefcase. "Oh, yes. Tom Walz mentioned you, Mr. Morrow. And if you want to talk about the faculty advisors meeting, I'm afraid there's nothing to discuss at this time."

She was a tough-looking woman, the kind of teacher Barry remembered avoiding all through his school days. "I want you to call off the meeting, Miss Archer."

She snorted softly, as if he were a four-year-old asking her to call off classes for the day. "There is a time and a place for everything, Mr. Morrow, and—"

"—and there are things you should know about Bill."

She gave him a quick glance, but continued sorting papers. "I think I know all I need to about Bill Sackter."

There was no point in trying to do battle with her, Barry reflected. People like Florence Archer thrived on confrontations. He drew the chair out and sat down. "I think I understand your feelings," he said sympathetically. "When I first met Bill I felt some of the same things you do. You're concerned about his presence on campus...even frightened of him, I imagine."

She glanced narrowly at him, suggesting that nothing frightened Florence Archer.

"And I think," Barry went on, "it's because you have no real knowledge of what sort of person Bill really is."

"You're right, I am concerned, Mr. Morrow. I don't think it is unusual to be wary of someone who is...mentally abnormal...when you have the responsibility for a group of children."

Barry sat forward, ready to meet her on her own ground. "What do the words 'normal' and 'abnormal' mean, Mrs. Archer? If you ran across Lee Harvey

Oswald, or James Earl Ray in the street, you would consider them normal. To you, Bill, who acts a bit odd, is abnormal. Yet there isn't a malicious bone in his body. What you are trying to do to him is far more destructive than anything he is capable of."

"My concern, Mr. Morrow," she said coolly, "is not how he appears today, but how he might act tomorrow. I think you made the point very well with Lee Harvey Oswald and James Earl Ray. No matter how harmless a person may appear he still might be a murderer or an assassin. Your friend Bill may appear harmless, but I doubt very much if you can predict his behavior at any moment."

Barry realized he'd made a mistake bringing up the names of assassins. "Mrs. Archer, Bill's been my friend for over a year now. I trust him with my child, and I've never doubted, in any way, the goodness of his heart. I feel about Bill the way you feel about your children. He won't change in the coming years as they will, but you can't devaluate his innocence and warmth."

He smiled, hoping it might disarm her a little. "That's what I love about Bill," he said. "He doesn't relate to the world the same way that we do. Look at us, we're always hurrying around from place to place trying to make a meeting or be a success, passing judgments on people. Bill doesn't give a damn about all that. All he cares about is friendship, having a good time with someone. Do you know why he came back to the playground after he'd been moved over to the Phys Ed Department?"

She didn't answer, but she stopped shoving papers around and looked at him.

"He came back because a little girl named Amy promised him a kitten. Bill had asked his landlady if he could have a kitten in the house, and when she said yes, he went over to the playground to tell Amy the good news. Does that sound like a murderer, or a rapist, or somebody who's going to run amuck and assault your children?"

She dropped her gaze to her papers, but said nothing.

"I don't know what's going to happen to Bill," Barry said. "But I do know he's found a home here at the University. For the first time in his life he's beginning to feel safe and wanted. And you have the power to take that away from him. I'm not asking you to help him, Mrs. Archer. All I'm asking is that you please don't hurt him."

The door opened behind Barry and an elderly man with a pipe came in. "Hello, Florence," he said, then glanced at Barry. "Am I interrupting something?"

"No, not at all," Florence said. She smiled faintly at Barry. "I think you've made your point, Mr. Morrow. I appreciate your coming to talk to me."

The next day Tom Walz was all smiles. Barry had gone through the cafeteria line and was searching the noisy dining room for an empty table when Walz called to him from the corner.

He was sitting with a tall, skinny man who appeared to be in his eighties. In spite of his age, the man was wearing a natty tweed jacket, and the twinkle in his eye suggested he felt more like thirty.

"Barry Morrow, this is Jonas Atkins," Walz said. "Sit down and join us. Barry Morrow is our hero, Jonas," he said to the older man. "He strode fearlessly into the cage and tamed the lioness. I don't know how he did it, but she was as gentle as a lamb."

Barry shook the older man's hand and sat down. "She wasn't very gentle when I left. What'd she say in the meeting?"

"Oh, she was all very businesslike," Walz said with a laugh. "She read all the rules and regulations concerning hiring requirements for University personnel, and then she talked about Bill Sackter and how he was totally unfit to be an employee. Then she went on about this being a very dangerous precedent, and warned us what disastrous consequences it might have for the future. All very grim and foreboding up to that point. But before we took any drastic actions, she suggested that we consider the possible consequences for Bill. It was not his fault that the rules had been broken, and after all he was a man with feelings and needs the same as the rest of us. Bill Sackter was mentally retarded, she said, but that did not mean he is dangerous in any way. He is simply childlike and thus must be given all the consideration we give children. She then proposed that we not rush into discharging him, but that we allow ample time to find suitable employment for him elsewhere. She then proposed that Thomas Walz be a committee of one to undertake that task. The proposal was seconded, and passed unanimously."

Jonas Atkins smiled at Barry. "You should be in politics, young man. You could have a brilliant future."

"No, thanks," Barry said.

Walz chuckled. "Don't dismiss the suggestion too quickly, Barry. It came from one of the leading practioners of the art."

"Ex-practioner," Atkins corrected.

Barry looked at the man, but the face was not familiar. Tom Walz filled him in.

"Jonas was once the Mayor of Iowa City," he said. "He was also a city councilman and a state legislator, and a congressman for fourteen years. And he's been teaching government and political science here for the last twenty years. He's retiring in a couple of weeks."

Atkins laughed dryly. "Twenty years too late, according to some of the people around here. Eighty-three year old men are supposed to be out in the pasture munchin' grass."

Barry suspected he was a lot better than some of the teachers who were in their vigorous thirties and forties. The vigor was too often directed toward maneuvering their ways up the administrative ladder.

"So how's the search going to find a new home for Bill?" Walz asked.

"Not very well," Barry said. He told them about their visit to Elm Ridge, and Bill's artful sabotage of the whole thing. "It's getting close to the deadline, and it looks like Bev and I might have to take Bill in for a while." He told them about Bill's dishwashing and coffeemaking and vacuuming in his efforts to forestall disaster. "He just doesn't understand the whole situation," he concluded, "and I'm afraid he's in for a big shock when they run him out."

"Bill knows how to make coffee?" Walz asked, as if it were a major accomplishment.

"Yes, and he's very good at it. Apparently Kenny taught him."

"Huh," Walz grunted. Then he turned and explained the whole situation to Atkins.

"Is that Mae Driscoll over on Taylor Street?" Atkins asked when he finished.

"Yes. Do you know her?"

Atkins chuckled and sipped his coffee. "I haven't seen Mae Driscoll for twenty years. But I knew her father very well. Old Clarence Driscoll was quite a guy. Used to have the International Harvester agency in town. But that was way back before the Depression. Like the rest of us, he went broke when the hard times came. Sold auto parts for a while before he died."

It was a small world. "I guess Mae's father also took in boarders," Barry said.

"Oh, yes," Atkins said. "Old Clarence was a good churchgoer. He really believed in Christian charity, and that a man ought to practice what he preached. Sometimes he had as many as twenty hobos and tramps livin' out there in his barn. Anybody who didn't have enough to eat could always get a meal from Clarence. And if they were crippled or couldn't work for one reason or another, he'd give 'em a place in the house and they could stay on as long as they wanted. A lot of people in town didn't like that much. I remember one old busybody, Mrs. Armquist, came down to City Hall and demanded we put a stop to it."

"Were you on the City Council at the time?" Barry asked.

"That's right." Atkins squinted an eye toward the windows. "Let's see, that must have been around nineteen thirty-four or so. About the first term I served." He laughed. "It was my introduction into the world of practical politics. It was when I gave up working and became a professional politician. It was a lot easier than practicing law. 'Course back in those days the City Council didn't amount to much. Luke Schnitzer was the Mayor. He also had a barbershop over on Fourth Street. So most of the council meetings were sort of informal affairs in Luke's backroom. Sometimes they went on past midnight, and sometimes there was so much city business, it interfered with our poker games. Mrs. Armquist didn't think much of that either." He laughed again. "But that's where we made up all the statutes and ordinances for the city. Then we'd meet at City Hall the next morning and take about ten minutes to vote and make everything legal and legitimate."

Barry smiled, thinking how different things were today. It was hard to say which system was better. "Mae Driscoll said something about a council resolution concerning her father's boardinghouse."

"That's right," Atkins said with a laugh. "Mrs. Armquist pestered us so much, we had to put a stop to it. So we had a poker game and Luke Schnitzer made up a resolution saying Clarence Driscoll was a law-abiding man, and if he wanted to act like a Christian, that was his business, and no matter how evil or Satanic any other citizens thought those practices were, the City Council would abide by the United States Constitution and support his right to do whatever he wanted in practicing his religion. I'm not sure how the wording went, but it was something like that. Old Luke had a droll sense of humor. So we met the next morning and made it official, and that was the end of Mrs. Armquist's huffing and puffing."

"I wish it were that simple today," Barry said.

Atkins agreed. "Yes, those were the good old days. Everybody hungry and everybody nice to each other. And some of those laws Luke made up were real classics." Atkins frowned thoughtfully at the table. "Maybe that's what I'll do after I retire; go down there to City Hall and dig out all those old ordinances. They ought to make an interesting collection."

He suddenly looked at his watch and rose. "Well, I got a class in about three minutes. Nice to meet you, Mr. Morrow."

Tom Walz shook his head as Atkins walked out the door. "I hate to see him retiring. He knows more about how government works than all the textbooks in the library."

"Why is he retiring?" Barry asked.

"Because there are too many people like Florence Archer around here. It wouldn't matter if you were Albert Einstein and Albert Schweitzer rolled into one, you're supposed to be useless after you reach sixty-five or seventy. Atkins has lasted a lot longer because he's such a good politician. He convinced all the administrators they were geniuses and saints for letting him stay."

Barry smiled and stirred his coffee. "As a committee of one to find Bill a new job, have you come up with any ideas."

Walz shook his head. "A few glimmers, but they may take some manipulating."

Barry nodded, hoping Tom Walz was as good a politician as Jonas Atkins.

After he finished the hallway upstairs, Bill carried the vacuum cleaner down to the living room and plugged the wire into the socket behind Mae's chair. Mae was wearing her thick glasses today, studying the classified section of the newspaper, carefully circling things with a red pen.

"You don't have to vacuum in here today, Bill," she said. "I just did it yesterday while you were at work."

Bill pushed the machine into the middle of the room and switched it on. "That's okay. I don't have anything else to do." He shoved it back and forth as if scrubbing the dirt away with a brush.

"Bill?"

He turned off the machine. "What?"

"What happened to the kitten you were gonna bring home?"

Bill turned away and switched the machine back on. "I don't know." He didn't want to talk about that with Mae. Amy had probably given the kitten to somebody else, and he would never see her again. But that was all right, he guessed. It would be hard to vacuum the carpets if there was a kitten around.

"Bill?"

"What?" He switched the machine off again.

Mae set the newspaper aside and pulled herself out of the chair. "Somebody's at the door."

Bill followed her across the room and into the entry hall. When she opened the door a tall man wearing a long beard and a black suit and hat was standing outside. He looked very sad as he took his hat off and smiled at them.

"You from the Housing Authority?" Mae asked him.

The man shook his head. "No, m'am. I am Rabbi Portman. I'm looking for a man named Bill Sackter. Have I come to the right address?"

"This is the right address," Mae said. "And this is Bill Sackter. Why don't you come on in?"

"Thank you." The man came in and extended his hand to Bill. "How do you do, Mr. Sackter."

"Glad to meetcha," Bill said.

"Mr. Sackter, I wonder if I might have a word with you?"

"Sure. All you want," Bill said.

Kenny and Angela suddenly appeared from the kitchen. The Rabbi glanced uneasily at them, then put his hand on Bill's elbow and guided him into the living room. "May I sit down?"

"Sure," Bill said. They both sat down while Mae herded Kenny and Angela back into the kitchen.

The Rabbi sat with his hat in his lap and studied it for a minute. When he looked up he seemed to be very unhappy. "Mr. Sackter, I'm afraid I have very sad news for you."

"Then I don't want to hear it," Bill said. He started to rise.

"Please," the Rabbi said. "It's about your sister."

Bill's heart jumped. "About Sarah? I don't want to hear any sad news about Sarah. I've got lots of work to do."

"I'm sorry, Bill. Her heart just gave out. Sarah died yesterday."

Bill felt his throat clog up, then tears burst out of his eyes and streamed down his cheeks. Sarah was his sister, and she was the only sister he had. There was nobody else in the world that he remembered from when he was little. He sniffled to keep the tears from filling his nose. "I hate nursing homes," he said. "I was saving my money to go to Florida to see her. I was going to take care of her."

"Yes . . . well, I'm sure they did the best they could, Bill."

Bill found a handkerchief in his pocket, and the rabbi waited until he had dried his eyes. Then the man reached into his coat pocket and pulled out something wrapped in tissue paper. "Sarah sent this to you. She wanted you to have it. It belonged to your father."

Bill took the package and slowly unwrapped it. "What is it?" A star attached to a silver chain dropped into his lap.

"It's called the Star of David," the Rabbi said.

"Oh." Bill held it up and watched the star turn slowly around. "Is it like a medal?"

"It's a symbol of the Jewish religion," the Rabbi said. "You see, your father was Jewish. Didn't you know that?"

Bill shook his head. "No, I didn't know that. But I go to church. I go to church with Mae every Sunday. It's a Baptist Church, I think."

"That's fine, Bill. But if you would like to learn more about the Jewish religion, you can come to our Synagogue and talk to me any time you want. Here, I'll give you a card with the address on it. It's not very far from here."

Bill took the card. "Yes, I'd like to do that, Rabbi. I like to go to church. I'll come and talk to you some time. Some time real soon."

The rabbi smiled and stood up. "That's fine, Bill. I'll be looking forward to seeing you. And please, call me Jeff. Okay?"

"Okay...Jeff." Bill looked at the Star of David again, then realized the rabbi wanted to leave. He jumped to his feet and walked him to the door. "Thank you very much for coming," he said and opened the door.

The rabbi shook his hand again. "I'm sure Sarah is at peace now, Bill. She was very ill and suffered a great deal. But now she is resting comfortably. She is with God."

"Sure," Bill said. "She's with God now."

Bill closed the door and looked at his Star of David again. He had never heard anything about his father before. Now he knew something about him.

"Are you Jewish?" Angela asked from the kitchen door.

"Yes, I am," Bill said and started up the stairs. "I'm Jewish and Methodist and Baptist and Episcopal."

"You can't be all those things!" Angela shouted.

Bill reached the top of the stairs and went to his room. "Yes, I can!" he shouted back and closed the door. Then he burst into tears again.

XVI

On Monday morning, Bill was still depressed. He went to work and, as usual, started sweeping on the top floor and worked his way down the stairs of the building. But there was a great emptiness inside of him, as if some part of him was gone forever. The students smiled and said hello, and gave him pats on the back. But Bill wouldn't bring himself to do anything more than nod in return.

When noon came, he picked up his lunchpail and started walking aimlessly across the campus, not feeling hungry at all. He walked past the administration building and past the Social Work building, and finally around to the playground where he used to talk to Amy.

The children were sitting on the benches under the trees, eating their lunches. Bill sat down on the grass and watched them from a distance, trying to spot Amy among them. He couldn't find her. Maybe she was eating her lunch in the classroom. Or maybe she hadn't come to school today.

The teacher sitting with the children was not Miz Archer. She was much younger and looked like one of the college students. Bill pulled himself up and walked slowly forward, ready to turn away if Miz Archer suddenly appeared. When he reached the edge of the playground he hesitated, then shuffled slowly over to the young teacher.

"Hello," she said and smiled at him.

Bill smiled and nodded. "Hello. My name is Bill. Where is Amy today?"

The teacher's face darkened. "Amy is sick, Bill. She's very sick."

"Sick?" Bill stopped breathing for a moment, remembering Rabbi Portman saying the same thing about his sister Sarah. "Where is she?"

"She's at the University Hospital. She's been there for three days now."

"Oh," Bill said. He didn't know what more to ask the young lady, and he didn't know what to do. He stared at the swings and slides for a minute, and then nodded at the teacher. "Thank you very much," he murmured, and walked away.

She was going to give him a kitten, he thought to himself. And now she was sick. The teacher had said she was very sick, the same as Sarah. Bill felt tears forming in his eyes.

The phone was ringing when Barry walked into his office on Tuesday morning. He was carrying a stack of film cans in one hand, and a briefcase and three books in the other. He dropped the briefcase and books on the desk and hurriedly picked up the receiver. "Hello?"

It was Bev. "Honey, two minutes after you left this morning, Mae Driscoll called. Apparently Bill didn't come home last night?"

"What?!"

"She just discovered it this morning. She and all the others had gone to bed early last night, and when she went to wake Bill this morning his bed was empty, and it hadn't been slept in."

"Has she called the police?"

"Yes, but they haven't seen him."

"Was he home for dinner last night?"

"No. And Mae said he was very quiet when he went to work yesterday morning. She figured he was upset about his sister. Did you know she died last week?"

"No, I didn't. Did he say anything about going anywhere?"

"No, but he was talking about a kitten. Apparently somebody was going to give him a kitten, but he never brought it home."

His kitten! Barry remembered how upset he was about Florence Archer keeping him away from the playground, and the little girl who was going to give him a kitten. What was the girl's name? Emily? Audrey? Something like that. "Okay," Barry said, "I'll see if he's anywhere around the campus, and then I'll call Mae."

He put the film cans on a shelf and checked his watch. There was still an hour and a half before his first class. He strode out of the office and down the stairs and headed across the campus toward Florence

Archer's classroom. It was a surprise about Bill's sister, Sarah, and probably very bad news for Bill. When things got rough for him, he always brought up Sarah, as if she were his lifesaver in any disaster. Barry hoped desperately that the old guy hadn't headed for Florida.

Florence Archer wasn't in the classroom. A younger teacher, a pretty girl with oversized glasses, was leading the children in a song. Barry quietly slipped through the door and waited until they were finished. The girl came smiling over to the door.

"I'm sorry to interrupt," Barry said, "but have you seen Bill Sackter around here in the last day or two? He's kind of a short funny-looking guy who wears odd hats."

"Yes, I saw him yesterday. He was asking about Amy Hill."

"Did he talk to her?"

The girl shook her head. "No. Amy's been in the University Hospital for several days. When I told Bill, he seemed rather upset."

"Why is she in the hospital?"

"She has spinal meningitis. I'm afraid she's in serious condition."

"Oh, my God," Barry groaned. "Well...thanks." He pulled the door open and slipped out again.

He was sitting in the far corner of the lobby, slumped in a chair with his gaze fixed vacantly on the floor. The receptionist watched Barry cross toward him and smiled, as if relieved. Barry sat down in the chair beside him, but Bill didn't notice. He appeared to be half asleep.

"Bill?"

"Oh, hi, Barry." He lifted his head for a moment, then fixed his gaze on the floor again.

"Have you been here all night, Bill?"

"Yes," he said woozily, "I've been here all night. But that's okay. I'm all right."

"Why didn't you tell Mae where you were going? She's worried sick about you."

"She'll understand," he murmured.

Barry sighed and glanced around the lobby. Only three other people were there, all of them reading magazines. "Listen, Bill, Amy Hill is very sick. She's got a disease called spinal meningitis. It's a very bad disease. But there's nothing you can do for her here. She may be here for days. Why don't you let me take you home?"

"That's okay, I'll stay," he said.

"Bill, you're not going to be able to see her. Only her mother and father are allowed in."

"I'll wait," he said.

Barry sat back in the chair and let out a long breath. He couldn't physically pick up Bill and carry him out of there. So what other choices did he have? He wondered if Amy Hill's parents were upstairs. He gave Bill a pat on the knee and pulled himself out of the chair. "I'll be back in a couple minutes, Bill."

The receptionist told him the floor, and he took the elevator up. It emptied him in front of a floor nurse's desk. "Yes," the gray-haired nurse said. "Mr. and Mrs. Hill are in the waiting room just around the corner."

They were the only people there. Mr. Hill was a gaunt man in a gray business suit. His tie was loosened and he was bent forward rubbing his forehead. His wife was plump, but attractive, wearing a heavy black coat. She was sitting on the couch, gazing numbly at the windows.

Barry introduced himself and quietly explained the situation, telling them how fond of Amy Bill was, and how long he had been sitting in the lobby. Would it be all right if Bill visited Amy for five minutes or so?

Both of them appeared to be too shattered to give the question any serious thought. Barry quietly pled his case some more, suggesting that it couldn't do any harm and perhaps might be good for Amy.

166

Mrs. Hill finally smiled and nodded. "All right," she said. "Amy's been unconscious for some time, but if it will help the man, that's fine."

He brought Bill up on the elevator, and the floor nurse smiled and nodded and told them the room number. Bill removed his hat and tiptoed down the hall and through the open door. Barry leaned on the door-post and waited outside.

Bill walked over to the bed and stood looking at the little girl for several minutes. "Hi, Amy," he finally whispered.

The girl's eyes were closed and she was breathing heavily. Bill carefully eased down on a chair next to the bed, still watching her. Then he lowered his head and folded his hands on his lap. Tears trickled down his cheeks.

"Our Father Who art in Heaven," he said chokingly, "hallowed be Thy name...kingdom come...Thy will be done...earth as Heaven. Help bring powers to heal my little friend, Amy. Please, God, don't let her hurt. Bless her, Lord. Rock of Ages. Amen."

Barry felt his own throat thicken. He turned away and walked slowly down the hall.

It was hard to say if Bill's prayers were a factor in Amy's recovery. But three days later, Mrs. Hill left a message at Mae Driscoll's house saying Amy was being released from the hospital and looked forward to seeing Bill in a week or two.

As the deadline from the Housing Authority drew closer, Barry abandoned any hopes of finding a new home for Bill. Along with Jack Wynhart, he had canvassed every possibility in town. Short of putting him in an institution, there was no other choice but to move him into the apartment.

Bev and Barry rearranged furniture, and Barry moved most of his film and tape equipment into a corner of the living room. Until they could think of something better, Bill would share a bedroom with Clay, and they would make whatever adjustments were necessary as problems arose.

Barry resigned himself to this awkward solution, and then, three days before the deadline, Tom Walz delivered some news to Barry that made the situation even more depressing.

Barry had just finished with his eleven o'clock class and was opening his bag lunch when Walz called and invited him to meet him in the faculty dining room. It was not an invitation so much as a command, as Tom Walz refused to accept any excuses. "I'll see you there in fifteen minutes," he said cheerfully, and hung up.

Tom was sitting by himself and looking at the menu when Barry arrived. He grinned broadly and shook Barry's hand and then called the waitress as quickly as Barry sat down.

"Well, how do you like teaching so far?" he asked after the waitress had left.

Barry smiled at the question. He had been too busy to give it much thought one way or the other. "I like it," he said. "I like it very much. In fact I think it's very helpful to me. The kids are so full of ideas, it's very stimulating."

Walz nodded and toyed with his fork. From the twinkle in his eye, he obviously was ready to spring something. "Would you be terribly upset if you had to give it up?"

What did he mean by that? Was Barry going to be fired? Promoted? Transferred? "Well, that depends, I guess," he said noncommittally.

Walz nodded and put the fork down. "I hope you don't mind, but I took the liberty of sending your tapes of Bill to some people I know. Some people out in California."

Barry stared at him. "What kind of people?"

"Uh ... some friends. Some people who happen to be in the movie and television production business."

"No," Barry said. "I don't mind at all. When did you send them?"

"About three weeks ago. They're a couple of young fellows who went to school here about ten years ago. One of them is now the executive vice-president of an independent film company. The other one is an editor in one of the big studios."

"Oh," Barry said. He was almost afraid to ask the next question. "Have you heard anything?"

"Yes, I've heard from both of them. They both liked the material very much. In fact the one at the film company wants you to come out to California and go to work for him. He wants you to start in the editing department, then do some second-unit production work—whatever that is."

Barry was so excited, he could hardly speak. "When?"

"As soon as possible."

"But I can't," Barry stammered. "I mean I've got a contract with the University."

Walz grinned. "No problem there. It's only two weeks to the end of the term. Then I can fire you."

"Fire me?"

"Sure. Incompetence, being late to classes, any reason you want. Or you can just quit. Nobody'll complain about the contract."

Barry suddenly loved Tom Walz more than any man on earth. But then, just as suddenly, another dark cloud materialized on the horizon. Barry shook his head. "I can't do it, Tom."

"Why not?"

"Bill," he said simply. "He's being evicted at the end of the week, and he has no place to go. Bev and I are taking him in."

Walz shrugged. "So, take him to California with you."

"I can't. A part of the deal with the welfare office in Minnesota is that Bill does not leave Iowa. They were pretty firm about that."

"Couldn't you talk to them, tell them the circumstances?"

Barry thought about it, then shook his head. "They won't buy it. I've hardly gotten him settled here, and then I ask to take him to California. They want him close to home where they can keep an eye on him. I'm afraid Iowa is about the limit."

"And there's no other place you could put him?"

Barry sighed, thinking about all the phone calls he had made, and his visit to Elm Ridge. "No. No place that I'd feel comfortable leaving him."

Their lunch arrived and Walz picked up his fork. "Well, I admire your selflessness in sticking with him. And maybe the job offer will still be around when you're ready to go."

They ate in silence for a minute, and Barry resisted the temptation to ask for more details about the job offer. Why torture himself? "Speaking of jobs," he finally asked, "have you come up with any ideas for Bill?"

Walz narrowed his eyes and looked thoughtful as he pushed his food around. "Maybe. I'm still doing some manipulating. Things might be worked out in a week or so. I'll let you know."

On the final night before their departure from the boardinghouse, Mae cooked dinner as usual, and they all ate in the kitchen without mentioning the fateful morning that was fast approaching.

"I'll wash the dishes," Bill volunteered when they were finished.

'No," Mae said and gathered up the plates. "You've done enough dishes in the last few weeks. We're just gonna let 'em set, because I got a special dessert for you all."

It was Mae's specialty: a German chocolate cake with a big scoop of vanilla ice cream on the side. Normally Angela always pointed out that the treat

170

contained far more calories than any of them should have. Tonight she said nothing.

"It sure is good," Bill said. "You make real good cake, Mae."

"Thank you very much," Mae said in a perfect imitation of Bill's favorite phrase. Bill grinned and Angela and Kenny giggled.

"Why don't you give your dolly some, Angela?" Kenny suggested.

Angela shook her head and turned the doll around in her lap. "She's too fat already."

They finished their dessert in silence, and carried the dirty plates to the sink. "Just leave them there," Mae said. "Let's just all go into the living room and sit down. Is there anything good on television, Bill?"

"I don't want to watch TV," Bill answered, and the others agreed.

"All right, then we'll just go sit and talk. That'll be real nice for a change."

Mae sat in the middle of the sofa, and Bill and Kenny sat beside her. Angela took the rocking chair, and held her doll close to her breast as she rocked back and forth.

"Well, is everybody all packed and ready?" Mae asked. "Barry said he'll be here promptly at ten o'clock tomorrow, so we don't want to keep him waiting."

"I don't wanta go to that Elm Ridge Nursing Home," Angela said petulantly. "I don't like that lady, and I don't like the room."

Mae smiled sympathetically. "I know, dear, but I'm sure you'll make lots of new friends there. And they have lots of things to do."

Angela's face contorted in her effort to hold back tears. "I don't want to do lots of things. I want to stay here with Bill and Kenny." She looked at Bill, then lowered her head, blinking away her tears. "I'm real sorry about all the mean things I said to you, Bill. I like you very much, and I like Kenny too. You're my best

171

friends, and I like you a lot. I like you both better than anybody in the world."

Bill stared at her, feeling his throat tighten. "I like you too, Angela. And I'd rather stay here, too."

"Now, now, Bill," Mae said. "You're going to live with Barry and Bev and Clay, and that's going to be real nice. They've been real good to you."

"I know," Bill said and sniffled. "I like them very much. But I like it here better. I liked living with you and Kenny and Angela."

Mae patted his hand and looked at Kenny. "And Kenny, you've got to get over your shyness. That's a nice resident hotel you're going to, but they don't have any work for you there. So you're going to have to go out and get a job somewheres else."

"Okay," Kenny said, but he wrung his hands and stared anxiously at the carpet.

"And you can help out Barry and Bev, the same as you've been doing here, Bill," Mae said and squeezed Bill's hand. "You've been real good here, and Bev will sure appreciate your doing chores around her place, too."

Bill didn't want to talk about that. "What are you going to do?" he asked Mae.

"Well, now, don't you worry none about me. I'm puttin' this old house up for sale next week, and I'll be out of here quick enough. Then I'll find some place to live where I can come and visit all three of you as often as I can."

Angela couldn't hold back the tears any longer. She clutched her doll and curled forward and sniffled while the tears streamed down her cheeks. Then she dropped to the floor, crawled across the carpet and dropped her head in Mae's lap.

"Now, now," Mae said soothingly, "it's going to be all right, Angela." She stroked Angela's head and tried to hold back her own tears.

Bill felt his stomach quivering, and he sniffled and rubbed his sleeve across his nose. He wondered why all this was happening, and why people were being mean to him and Mae and Angela and Kenny. They hadn't done anything bad to anybody. He felt Mae's arm around him, and he dropped his head on her shoulder.

Mae had her other arm around Kenny, and then they were all crying and holding tightly to each other.

"It's gonna be all right," Mae said quietly, "it's gonna be all right. No matter where we go, we're all just gonna keep on lovin' each other."

XVII

The final morning arrived under a gloomy shroud of gray sky that promised rain or snow at any moment. Barry showered and shaved and read the morning paper while he ate breakfast, all the while trying not to think about the task ahead of him. The Middle East was still boiling with turmoil, the OPEC ministers were threatening to raise oil prices again, El Salvador and all of Central America was on the brink of disaster, and Barry Morrow's life was about to take a long backward step.

"It'll work out all right," Bev said as she got him another cup of coffee. "It's really not the end of the world."

"I suppose not," Barry agreed. He hadn't told her about the offer from the film company in Hollywood. There was no point in her becoming depressed also.

She sat down and smiled in an effort to raise his spirits. "I bought some new sheets for Bill's bed. And maybe we ought to get some kind of a rack, or maybe a pegboard to Bill's hats. I don't think the landlord would appreciate his pounding nails into the walls."

"Okay," Barry sighed. "I'll see if I can find something this afternoon."

"It's really not going to be so bad. And we'll have a built-in baby sitter when we want to go out."

Barry appreciated her efforts. But no matter which way you looked at it, it was going to be difficult for them and for Bill. And the most frustrating part of the situation was that Bill was far happier living with Mae than he was going to be in their apartment. Barry checked his watch. "I'd better get going. Angela's got a whole room full of dolls and doll houses. I'll have to make two trips to get her out to that nursing home."

He put on his jacket and was at the bottom of the stairs when Bev suddenly called out to him.

"There's a man named Atkins on the phone," she said. "Shall I tell him you've gone?"

"Did he say what he wants?"

"No, he just asked for you. Do you know him?"

Barry stood indecisively for a moment, then climbed the stairs again. "Yeah, he's a nice old guy who teaches political science." He couldn't imagine why Jonas Atkins was calling him on a Saturday morning. He certainly wasn't looking for a golf partner on a day like this. Barry picked up the phone.

"Hello, Mr. Atkins. How are you?"

"Just fine, just fine," the raspy old voice answered. "I'm sorry to disturb you, Barry, but I'm looking at something you might be interested in. I'm down here at the City Hall, and I think you ought to come on down and have a look."

Barry was in no mood to play games. "What is it, Mr. Atkins? I'm kind of busy this morning."

"Well, it's about Mae Driscoll and her boarding-house. Didn't you say something about the Housing Authority kicking out her tenants pretty soon now?"

"This is their last day," Barry said. "I'm moving them all out this morning."

"Well, now, that might not be necessary at all. I think you ought to come down here right away, Barry. It shouldn't take you long, and I'll be waitin' for you in the City Attorney's office. It's on the fourth floor."

Barry's heart thudded against his ribs. But he cautioned himself not to get his hopes up. "Okay, I'll be there in ten minutes." He dropped the phone in the cradle and stared silently at it for a minute.

"What is it?" Bev asked.

"I don't know. Jonas Atkins was on the City Council about fifty years ago; back when Mae Driscoll's father had some trouble with the boardinghouse. He says maybe Bill and the others won't have to move after all."

Bev brightened. "Really? You think it's possible?"

Barry shook his head and crossed to the door again. "I don't know. But I don't think we'd better count on it."

The sky looked better as Barry drove downtown. The big black clouds were moving steadily eastward and there were patches of blue in the west. He drove faster than usual through the light traffic, and easily found a slot in the almost empty parking lot.

He took the elevator to the fourth floor and followed a broad corridor to the imposing door at the end that said *City Attorney*.

"Mr. Greer is expecting you," the girl at the desk said, and Barry continued on through another impressive door.

There were three people in the office. The man behind the desk was in his mid-thirties; handsome and energetic-looking, with a styled haircut. He was in his shirtsleeves, and he smiled and rose and stuck a hand across the desk. "Mr. Morrow, it's nice to meet you. I'm Harold Greer."

In addition to Jonas Atkins, Jack Wynhart was sitting in one of the leather chairs in front of the desk. Both men were smiling.

"Sit down, Mr. Morrow," the attorney said after Barry shook his hand. Then the man settled into his chair and frowned at a piece of paper on his desk. "Do

175

you want to tell him about this, Jonas?" he said to Atkins, "or do you want me to do it?"

"Be my guest," Atkins said. "You're the expert."

Greer nodded and brought his hands together, making a little steeple in front of his face. "Mr. Atkins brought me a document this morning," he said. "A rather ancient document, as a matter of fact. It's dated May 12, 1935. It seems to be a resolution relating to the Driscoll house on Taylor Street, and it was passed unanimously by the City Council on that date. By the wording, however, it appears to be far more than a resolution. In my opinion, it has all the elements necessary to make it an official ordinance. Without going into all the legal technicalities involved, Mr. Morrow, I would say that this is a legal document establishing certain rights and privileges for the owner of the Driscoll house on Taylor Street—rights and privileges that cannot be withdrawn or cancelled."

"What kind of rights?" Barry asked.

"Well...perhaps I should read the resolution to you." The man smiled faintly and picked up the paper. "You'll find this a bit more colorful than the language used by the present City Council." He cleared his throat.

"'Be it known to all citizens of Iowa City, and to any and all visitors to this fair city, that the duly elected members of this Council have thoroughly examined the premises, the operation and the character of the so-called boardinghouse run by Clarence J. Driscoll on Taylor Street of this city, and we have found it to be a model of cleanliness and Godliness, and we have found the owner and his family to be of irreproachable character, and to be admirable examples of loving, charitable Christians. And although certain citizens of this community may find cleanliness, Godliness, love, charity and Christianity to be unattractive virtues, this Council cannot and will not interfere with Mr. Clarence J. Driscoll's constitutional right to practice his religious convictions in whatever manner he chooses.

"'Therefore, let it be resolved that the Driscoll boardinghouse shall be permitted to continue operating, and shall be exempt from all laws and ordinances which might in any manner interfere with that operation, and that this permit and the aforementioned exemptions shall continue in effect so long as any member of the Driscoll family continues to reside in the aforementioned house.'"

Greer set the paper down and smiled. "As a formal legal document, it's a little shaky. But I don't think a judge would have any trouble figuring out what it means." He glanced at Wynhart. "Do you think your department will want to challenge this in court, Jack?"

"I don't think so," Wynhart said. "We have no desire to close up the place."

"How about the plumbing and the number of bathrooms?" Barry asked.

Greer shrugged. "It seems clear to me that any ordinances concerning plumbing or bathroom requirements would interfere with Mae Driscoll's operation, and therefore could not be enforced."

For the first time, Barry smiled and eased back in his chair. He looked over at Jonas Atkins. "Thanks, Mr. Atkins."

Atkins held up a protesting hand. "No thanks are required. I am merely an ordinary citizen anxious to see that all the laws are obeyed. And obviously it was the will of the people that the Driscoll boardinghouse continue operating."

"May I have a copy of that document?" Barry asked.

Greer smiled and reached into his desk. "I rather suspected you would want one." He handed over a xeroxed copy.

Barry felt like leaping up and kicking his heels together as he bounded down the steps of the City Hall. Bill and Angela and Kenny could stay in the boardinghouse. And—assuming that Tom Walz could find a job for Bill—Barry could accept the job in Hollywood.

"Are you sure about this?" Mae asked.

"I'm sure the City Attorney said you have the legal right to run a boardinghouse here as long as you live," Barry told her.

Barry had marched them all into the kitchen and sat them down at the table before he announced the good news. Kenny stared suspiciously at him, and Bill and Angela looked bewildered.

"I don't have to go to the nursing home?" Angela asked.

"Not as long as Mae wants you here," Barry answered. "And you too, Bill. You can stay as long as you want."

Bill nodded solemnly. "I'm going to stay."

"Me too," Kenny agreed.

"Well, let's all thank the Lord," Mae said. "He's sure enough answered our prayers. And thanks to Barry, and to that nice Mr. Atkins. It just shows, doesn't it, that there are still nice people in the world. And now I think I'll just make a fresh pot of coffee."

Bill leaped to his feet before she could move. "I'll make it. I'm real good at it now." He was at the stove in two strides, a broad grin across his face.

They had all moved their things down to the living room, ready to load them into the station wagon. When they finished their coffee, Barry helped them move everything back to the rooms. Compared to the gloom that must have prevailed while they hauled everything down, the atmosphere was like a party now. Even Angela was laughing as she danced each of her dolls up the stairs.

Two weeks later, Bill had a new job. Barry hadn't heard a thing about it until Tom Walz came striding up behind him one afternoon and grasped his arm, propelling him along.

"I've been looking all over for you," he said with a grin. "I want to show you something. And then we've got to get Bill over here before he catches the bus home tonight."

Barry had been so wrapped up in looking at his students' films during the past week, he hadn't given a thought to Bill, or to Tom Walz's efforts to find Bill a job. Final exam week was starting and there was a subdued atmosphere of anxious tension around the campus.

"Is something on fire?" Barry asked. Walz was hustling him toward the Social Work building at full stride.

"I hope not," Walz answered. "But everything is going to work out fine for Bill. You *did* tell me he can make coffee, didn't you?"

"Yes."

"Good. Well, I pulled some strings and told some lies, and I wangled a little space for Bill. It used to be the storage room for the Registrar's records, and the fire department said it was unsafe."

"You mean that basement room?"

"Right. And once all those records were moved out, everybody on campus wanted the room for one thing or another. The Social Work professors wanted it for a faculty lounge and gym, and some of the other teachers wanted it for a counseling room, and somebody else wanted to turn it into a microfilm library. I told all of them that the fire department wouldn't go for it. Then I found an old coffee urn in back of the cafeteria, and an old cash register in the bookstore, and a bunch of chairs and tables in the storage room behind the faculty dining room. So I put them all together, and..."

"What are you talking about?" Barry asked. They had reached the steps leading into the sub-basement, and Walz grinned and guided Barry down.

"...and," Walz said, *"Voila!"*

Barry stopped at the door and gaped at the room

179

he had last seen covered with dust and littered with old cartons and papers. It now had a beamed ceiling and freshly painted walls with travel posters and college pennants, and eight or ten tables were arranged around a carpeted floor. At the far end was a counter with a case full of doughnuts and pastries, and an ancient cash register that looked like a museum piece. Behind the cash register was a gleaming coffee urn and stacks of crockery cups.

"What is it?" Barry asked.

"It's Wild Bill's Coffee Shop," Walz grinned. "A purely private enterprise licensed by the University, but subject to none of the University's hiring requirements. It is a haven for students, and a place where they can buy coffee from a regular good man who is making it on his own."

Barry laughed, suddenly feeling good inside. He knew Bill could handle it, and that it was exactly what he needed. At the far end of the counter he noticed a big chocolate cake with a single candle in it. "What's the cake for?"

"It's for Bill. And you've got exactly twenty minutes to find him and get him over here," Walz said. "We're having a little surprise celebration for him."

"Then I'd better see if I can find him."

Barry was amazed at how thoroughly Tom Walz had planned everything. He was even more amazed when he climbed the steps and found himself face-to-face with Mae Driscoll, who had Kenny and Angela in tow. Mae was wearing a red and green plaid dress, and a big hat covered with fruit.

"Oh, my," she said, "are we late?"

Angela was wearing her ruffles. Behind her, and glancing anxiously around as if expecting an Indian attack, Kenny was all dressed up in a blue suit and a tie.

"No, you're fine," Barry assured her. "Go on in. I'm going to find Bill."

Ten minutes later he found Bill leaning on his

broom, watching the basketball team practice. He was wearing a gray-striped engineer's cap and he was gawking at the basketball players as if he couldn't believe how fast they threw the ball around.

"Oh, hi, Barry," he said flatly.

"How you doing, Bill? Why don't you put your broom away and come have a cup of coffee with me?"

Bill frowned and looked at the broom. "Oh, I'm going to go home pretty soon. At five o'clock a bell rings, and then I have to catch the bus."

"That's okay," Barry said, "I'll drive you home tonight."

Bill nodded and they walked toward the exit. "Where are we having a cup of coffee, Barry?"

"I know a new place. But we'd better hurry."

Bill rarely moved faster than a snail's pace. But Barry kept him moving, angling across the campus and around the corner of the Social Work building.

The coast was clear, and Bill frowned as Barry led him down the four steps. "Why are we going down here?" he asked.

Barry said nothing and pulled the door open. It was dark inside, and Bill stopped, suddenly groping for Barry's arm. Then the lights came on.

"Surprise!!"

Bill gaped at the smiling people in disbelief. Dr. Walz was there. Mae and Angela and Kenny were there, all dressed up and smiling at him. Ed Jenkins, his boss was there, and four other men from the Maintenance Department. And Miz Archer was there too—and she was smiling! And next to Miz Archer was Amy, and she had a little kitten in her arms! And next to her was Rabbi Portman. And even Miss Keating from Minneapolis was there! Bill stared speechlessly at them, wondering why they were all there.

"You know what this means, Bill?" Dr. Walz asked as everybody clapped.

Bill shook his head. "What does it mean?"

"It means this room is now your permanent place

to work. From now on you're going to be a special consultant to the faculty and students."

Bill still didn't understand. "What does that mean?"

"All you have to do is make coffee and talk to the students."

Bill looked over at the coffee urn and the stacks of cups. He nodded. "I can do that."

Everybody clapped again, and Bill smiled at them.

"We're happy for you, Bill," Mae Driscoll said.

"Give us a speech, Bill," Ed Jenkins shouted out.

Bill frowned and looked at the floor. He scratched his nose with the back of his hand. He had never made a speech before. "Thank you very much," he said and nodded. "I've seen bad times. And these are the good times. Thank you very much." He felt tears coming into his eyes. "God bless you."

Tom Walz stepped in front of the others and raised his hands like a musical director. "For he's a jolly good fellow," he sang out, and the others quickly joined in. "For he's a jolly good fellow, for he's a jolly good fellow, which nobody can deny...."

Two weeks later, the students were all back on campus and another term was beginning. As excited as he was about going to California, Barry felt sad about leaving the University. He had enjoyed the challenge of teaching, and he had made so many friends among his students, he felt as if he were leaving home.

He waited until the day before they were scheduled to leave before he told Bill about their move to California. Bill was having such a good time running his new coffee shop that Barry didn't want to dampen his enthusiasm. But it had to be done, and on a Friday afternoon when there were only five or six students in the coffee shop, Barry walked in and drew a cup of coffee from the urn.

Bill was sitting with a pretty girl about eighteen, and was frowning hard with concentration, making marks on a yellow pad. Barry carried his cup across the room and joined them.

"Now dot the *i*," the girl said. "Just a tiny little dot is fine."

Instead of dotting the *i*, Bill straightened and looked at Barry, as if relieved by his arrival. "Hi, Barry," he said.

"Hi, Bill. I'm not gonna talk to you until you dot the *i*, buddy," Barry said. He winked at the girl, whose name was Carrie.

Bill's face darkened and he frowned at the paper again. He moved the pencil carefully to a position above the *i* and gave a quick peck at the paper.

"Perfect," Carrie said.

Bill smiled, pleased with himself. "I'm learning to write my name. This says *Bill*."

Barry chuckled. "You're gonna be a regular good man, huh?"

"A regular good man," Bill said and nodded.

Barry smiled at the girl. "Carrie, do you mind if I talk to Bill for a minute?"

"No." She glanced at her watch. "I've got to get going, anyway." She scooped up her books and rose. "See you on Monday, Bill."

"Thank you for helping me, Sweetie," Bill said as she left. He smiled at Barry. "She's a real sweetie. Just like Bev."

"So how you doin'?" Barry asked.

"I'm learning to write my name. And I'm going to the Synagogue and learning how to be Jewish. Jeff says I can have a bar mitzvah pretty soon."

"That's great, Bill." Barry took a deep breath and tried to sound casual. "Hey, guess what. I got some news. I was offered a new job. A better job. Only it's in a state far away."

It took Bill a minute to digest the words. Then his face darkened and he frowned at the pad in front of him. "How far?"

"Far," Barry said. "And...it'd mean we'd have to

183

move. That's what I wanted to talk to you about. What would you rather do—come with us, or stay here?"

Bill's chin dropped lower and he pushed at the yellow pad, then looked off in the other direction. When he turned back his face seemed to be full of pain. "I wouldn't hurt you for anything in the world," he said. "But I can't go with you. I have my job to do, too."

Barry stared at him, realizing that the only thing disturbing Bill was his fear of hurting his and Bev's feelings. "Bill, Bev and I . . ."

Bill shook his head. "My mind's all straight now, and I'm doing fine. I'll miss Clay."

"We'll all miss you," Barry said.

"And Sweetie."

Barry smiled. "Well, how about me?"

Bill nodded. "You're my buddy. I'll miss you too. But if you have a better job, you have to take it . . . 'cause you're movin' up, too, the same as me. There are two things in the world. One is: a man has to do what he's got to do. Right?"

"Yeah," Barry agreed. "What's the other thing?"

Bill frowned thoughtfully, then smiled. "I forget."

Barry laughed and gave him a pat on the back as he rose.

"Now, wait," Bill said. "If you're going away, I have to give you something." He pulled out his wallet and slid his two-dollar bill out of its slot. "Here."

"That's your lucky piece," Barry protested. "You can't give away your good luck."

Bill smiled and stuck the folded bill into Barry's shirt pocket. "Well, you're gonna need it, 'cause you're on your own now, too."

THE PRIVATE LIVES BEHIND PUBLIC FACES

These biographies and autobiographies tell the personal stories of well-known figures, recounting the triumphs and tragedies of their public and private lives.

☐	23809	**BLACK AND BLUE** Richard Pryor	$3.50
☐	05035	**OUT ON A LIMB** Shirley MacLaine (Hardcover)	$15.95
☐	23662	**"DON'T FALL OFF THE MOUNTAIN"** Shirley MacLaine	$3.50
☐	05020	**LIFE WITH JACKIE** Mansfield & Block (Hardcover)	$14.95
☐	23816	**THROUGH THE NARROW GATE** Karen Armstrong	$3.50
☐	05044	**GIANT STEPS** Kareem Abdul Jabbar & Peter Knobler (Hardcover)	$14.95
☐	20805	**ALWAYS, LANA** Pero and Rovin	$3.50
☐	20704	**BURIED ALIVE: The Biography of Janis Joplin** Myra Friedman	$3.95
☐	23886	**HAYWIRE** Brooke Hayward	$3.95
☐	23133	**'SCUSE ME WHILE I KISS THE SKY** David Henderson	$3.95
☐	20756	**MONTGOMERY CLIFT: A Biography** Patricia Bosworth	$3.95
☐	20857	**AN UNFINISHED WOMAN** Lillian Hellman	$3.50
☐	23005	**A SHINING SEASON** William Buchanan	$2.75

Prices and availability subject to change without notice.

Buy them at your local bookstore or use this handy coupon for ordering:

We Deliver!
And So Do These Bestsellers.

☐	23792	**THE COP WHO WOULDN'T QUIT** by Johnny Bonds & Rick Nelson	$3.95
☐	34035	**HOW TO SAVE A HEART ATTACK VICTIM** by Jack Froman, M.D.	$2.50
☐	23714	**THE DEVIL IN CONNECTICUT** by G. Brittle	$3.50
☐	22634	**THE AMITYVILLE HORROR** by Jay Anson	$3.50
☐	23695	**TOUGH LOVE** by P. & D. York w/ T. Wachtel	$3.50
☐	05042	**HEARTS WE BROKE LONG AGO** by M. Shain (A Large Format Book)	$10.95
☐	22646	**SOME MEN ARE MORE THAN PERFECT** by Merle Shain	$2.95
☐	22649	**WHEN LOVERS ARE FRIENDS** by Merle Shain	$2.95
☐	05035	**OUT ON A LIMB** by Shirley MacLaine (A Hardcover Book)	$14.95
☐	01457	**YOUR ACHING BACK** by A. A. White III, M.D. (A Hardcover Book)	$7.95
☐	23029	**HAVING IT BOTH WAYS** by E. Denholtz	$3.50
☐	23568	**GET A JOB IN 60 SECONDS** by Steve Kravette	$2.95
☐	23355	**'LUDES** by Benjamin Stein	$3.50
☐	22616	**THE DEMON SYNDROME** by Nancy Osborn Ishmael	$2.95
☐	23563	**THE ONLY INVESTMENT GUIDE YOU'LL EVER NEED** by Andrew Tobias	$3.95
☐	23188	**BEVERLY HILLS DIET LIFETIME PLAN** by Judy Mazel	$3.95
☐	22661	**UP THE FAMILY TREE** by Teresa Bloomingdale	$2.95
☐	22701	**I SHOULD HAVE SEEN IT COMING WHEN THE RABBIT DIED** by Teresa Bloomingdale	$2.75
☐	22576	**PATHFINDERS** by Gail Sheehy	$4.50
☐	22585	**THE MINDS OF BILLY MILLIGAN** by Daniel Keyes	$3.95
☐	22771	**THE GREATEST SUCCESS IN THE WORLD** by Og Mandino	$2.75
☐	23271	**WHY DO I THINK I'M NOTHING WITHOUT A MAN?** by Dr. P. Russianoff	$3.50

Prices and availability subject to change without notice.

Buy them at your local bookstore or use this handy coupon for ordering:

Bantam Books, Inc., Dept. NFB, 414 East Golf Road, Des Plaines, Ill. 60016

Please send me the books I have checked above. I am enclosing $_____ (please add $1.25 to cover postage and handling). Send check or money order —no cash or C.O.D.'s please.

Mr/Mrs/Miss_____

Address_____

City_____ State/Zip_____

NFB—1/84

Please allow four to six weeks for delivery. This offer expires 7/84.

SPECIAL
MONEY SAVING
OFFER

Now you can have an up-to-date listing of Bantam's hundreds of titles plus take advantage of our unique and exciting bonus book offer. A special offer which gives you the opportunity to purchase a Bantam book for only 50¢. Here's how!

By ordering any five books at the regular price per order, you can also choose any other single book in the catalog (up to a $4.95 value) for just 50¢. Some restrictions do apply, but for further details why not send for Bantam's illustrated Shop-At-Home Catalog today!

Just send us your name and address plus 50¢ to defray the postage and handling costs.